# The One True
# Magick

### The Powers of Enlightenment
### Through Meditation

## by
## Robert Sommers

TARNHELM PRESS
Lakemont, Georgia
USA

First Printing

Tarnhelm Press, Lakemont Ga. 30552

Library of Congress catalog card number: 75-41652

International Standard Book Number: 0-87707-161-6

Printed by CSA Printing & Bindery Inc.
Lakemont, Ga. 30552

# CONTENTS

## PREFACE

This book is an attempt to formulate a synthesis of western occultism, eastern philosophies, and other allied disciplines by offering the most essential points of each tradition. The goal of both western occultism and the eastern disciplines is self-realization, although this may not be apparent in the case of the former. Western occultism, like alchemy, should be understood symbolically, its operations interpreted as one would an anecdote. Although its values appear embedded in the materialistic world —its concerns being sexual satisfaction, wealth, and power—western ceremonial magic is also concerned with the growth and perfection of the individual. What is said of magic should not be taken only literally, but instead, its symbols should be regarded as representations of psychological processes and forces which are to be uncovered and mastered. The aspirant should think of magic's active and aggressive principles as a necessary complement to the east's passive and contemplative attitudes. The western occult traditions may be regarded as the yang, and eastern thought as the yin. Together these forces comprise the Tao; from their interaction arises creation.

By providing an overview of the diverse paths

to enlightenment, the author hopes to interest those of the western occult tradition in the ways of the east, and vice versa. At the same time, the theories and practices of the various disciplines are arranged to offer a comprehensive system of attainment for the beginner. In the search for Truth, one must explore all of the possibilities of one's being, all of the regions of the mind and body, and the many types of existence available.

Although he recognizes value in the different paths to enlightenment, the author's life is an expression of the principles of Zen. For this reason, the present book should be approached as a koan, a riddle provided to the aspirant as a tool for self-exploration. The solution to this riddle is self-realization. The purpose of this book is to force interested people to think for themselves, rather than accept any dogma as truth; for too often aspirants lean on dogma like a crutch, and this impedes progress instead of facilitating it. Hopefully, these writings will remove the aspirant's crutches and encourage in him a questioning and critical attitude. Out of this will emerge an abiding search for the Truth.

The ideas and practices of both the eastern philosophies and western occultism are means to an end, and should not be confused with the goal of self-realization. They describe phases of growth and in this way aid one towards self-discovery and self-mastery. When the goal of self-realization is reached the thoughts and exercises contained in this book become superfluous; these words are superseded by the coming into being of pure mind and action.

# INTRODUCTION

## I

This book was written in order to provide a guide for those aspirants who are truly desirous of mystical enlightenment. The book is arranged in progressive Grades in order to allow one to proceed gradually towards attainment. Furthermore, each Grade will contain helpful insights and hints to aid one with his understanding of the knowledge of the Grades, as well as with his practice of the exercises.

The Grades are subjective; each represents a viewpoint, and as such examines only certain aspects of Reality. However, when the Grade of Magister Templi is attained, one must have also attained objectivity. For it is the Magister Templi's obligation to teach others the Path; and to do this, he must realize that each aspirant is an individual and as such needs advice and practices peculiar to himself. Thus the Magister Templi cannot recommend one simple approach to Enlightenment. He must understand many and divers systems of attainment so that he may instruct all properly. For this reason, this book will introduce one to various truths and practices. However, it must be understood that no one book can contain a complete and thorough study of all the many systems of attainment. Therefore, this book will pro-

vide one with an over-all view of many systems in
the sense that it provides initiated insights into
many of the disciplines. It is assumed that the student will avail himself of many other sources of
knowledge as he realizes the need to study certain
doctrines more thoroughly.

## II

Strange as it may seem, I wish to discuss in
this introduction a problem which is not actually
confronted until quite some time later in one's
work. However, it is important to discuss it now
because it will lead to an examination of the very
real and practical aspects of pursuing enlightenment while living in the world.

The problem, which consists of how transcendental knowledge is applied to the gross everyday
world, revolves around the difference in meaning
between "knowing" and "realizing." Therefore, let
me first state that "knowing" refers to intellectual
knowledge such as is obtained through reading;
while "realizing" refers to direct, intuitive, experiencing as occurs due to actual practice.

In order to ever know transcendental knowledge, one must first realize it; that is, one must
directly, intuitively, experience it. For instance,
simply *reading* this book will not afford one much
help. In order to really understand what is said
one must meditate and perform the other practices
as instructed. However, having realized a bit of
transcendental knowledge, one may know (remember) it, when not still realizing it. That is, one may
experience a state of mind through meditation,

receive certain knowledge, and then remember this knowledge when no longer in the previously attained mental state. The implications of this, which are many and of the utmost importance follow:

Attaining Samadhi, one realizes "I am One with the Universal Consciousness; I am none other than the Creator." As such, one realizes everything as his own creations, or as illusions. Applying this knowledge to the world means terming the physical world, other bodies, other minds, other persons and animals, as illusions. One realizes that "I Alone Am Real." What then of human relationships?

We must now understand that realizing Samadhi and then remembering the experience and knowledge received is different than continuously realizing Samadhi. When one remains in Samadhi continuously, there is no perception of any problem because one is situated in the external transcendental Truth. But when one does not remain in Samadhi, it is then when he must reconcile the two worlds.

When no longer in Samadhi, understand that the transcendental, eternal Truth does not apply to one's material, transient world. For when not in Samadhi, one is again returned to the world of Illusion; and as one illusion to other illusions, we realize each other as real. Thus, when not in Samadhi, one knows the Truth, but realizes himself as real, and other people as real.

The question now asked is, "How can one know something to be the Truth, and yet not live by it?" The difference between "knowing" and "realizing" is accounted for by the ability of one to experience

Truth, but then be led away from following it by internal and external conditions. However, due to one's continuing practices of meditation, one experiences Samadhi more and more easily and for longer periods. In time, a point is reached where one can attain Samadhi at will, and this frees one completely. Thus after many lengthy experiences of Samadhi one acquires the strength of conviction to live according to the Truth. But until this stage is reached, the Truth is always slightly obscured by what we wish the Truth was, and also what we wish the Truth wasn't. On a gross level, one wishes he didn't have to die; but he knows that he must die. However, he doesn't have to commit suicide immediately in order to realize this turth. So also one may know the Truth, without yet desiring its complete realization. However, after many, many lifetimes, each person is gradually brought closer to the Truth, and finally he must face the Truth, and take up the Path in order to attain his ultimate destiny.

It appears absolutely incredible that there should be so many systems of attainment, or paths to enlightenment. But if we understand that each person, or individual consciousness of a certain level, can only experience certain truths, we understand the causes of this multiplicity of truths, (beliefs). Any truth which is not appropriate to one's level of consciousness will not be regarded as true. Therefore, there are many systems and truths, each appropriate for certain individuals. These systems and truths constitute the Grades. It is therefore one's most important task to ascertain his Grade by beginning and progressing as far as one is able. But the most important point to remember is that for each Grade, the corresponding facts are True. There is no doubt or disbelief. Those of higher Grades may write of facts of lower Grades as "truths" with a small "t," but to the man of that Grade, these same facts are undeniably the Truth.

## III

To one on the verge of continuous Samadhi, or eternally remaining one with God, the terrifying Truth which must be realized is that of being One; Alone With No Other.

To one who wishes to realize only a glimpse of Truth, only a moment of Samadhi, the terrifying Truth which must be realized is that of Non-self, or selflessness.

To one who wishes to realize only peace and contentment, the terrifying Truth which must be realized is that of Being; that everything is, and that no emotion may be attached to oneself. That is, one may not condone or condemn killing; one may not become outraged at acts of injustice; for whatever is, is right.

To one who wishes to gain only some insight or better health, the terrifying Truth which must be realized is that of Discipline. It is incredible that those who believe they wish for some sort of spiritual illumination, believe also that they already have such knowledge. They are told not to steal by the Master, and yet they do not understand the reason for the prohibition. This is no fancy of the Master; it is a prohibition because there is a valuable lesson to be learned therefrom. But those seeking enlightenment, believe that they know better than their teacher; they ask if it is acceptable to steal from the wealthy if they are poor? They are told "no." But they believe otherwise, and so they steal; though they persist in the other practices of Yoga. They ask if drugs lead one to God. They are told "no." Yet they believe otherwise, and so indulge in drug use, though they believe their teacher to be right in every other case! Basically, reationalizations and justifications allow such people to accept what they can and hope it's good enough. They deny what they can't accept and say it doesn't matter.

The above examples show two things: Firstly, one will believe as true, only what one will believe. Secondly, that there is no one system of attainment which is right for everyone; because due to differences in consciousness, each needs different experiences in order to advance toward enlightenment. But just as one will do whatever it is one will do, so through stealing or drug taking one may experience that which will lead to enlightenment, though in a way different than expected—"a fool who persists in his folly may in time become wise."

## IV

In the beginning, faith is essential; for without it, there is no reason to suppose that what are presented as truths, are in fact true. Likewise one must have faith in the practices, that they will succeed in providing one with true results. In time, and due to actual practice, these statements which follow are realized as true.

# I

## THE GRADE OF STUDENT

*The Need for Enlightenment*

Many people are confronted with the intellectual problem concerning the reason, or nature, of their existence. Philosophy, as an intellectual exercise, can aid one to solve this problem by providing the means and contents of an intellectual answer. An individual's intellectual answer to the question of his existence is a resultant of the forces which composed the question; that is, the intellectual solution is a logical working out of the intellectual problem. The power gained from an answer arrived at through such reasoning is experienced as peace and poise. However, another person's arguments can always introduce previously unconsidered factors, adding new forces to the question of one's existence. Our intellectual answer must be able to refute, incorporate, or in some way answer the intellectual arguments of others, in order for us to retain the peace and stability afforded by our intact philosophy. Thus, one may find oneself constantly thinking of new answers, constantly refining his philosophy, constantly expanding his philosophy. Plagued by the need to explain factors introduced by others, one is continuously besieged by new spasms of thought. Thus, we lose some of the peace conferred by our philosophy.

Another way of answering the intellectual question concerning one's existence is the mystical experience. This method, rather than formulating an intellectual answer for an intellectual question, results in the elimination of the intellectual question altogether. Thus, the attainment of Zen is the annihilation of our tendency towards intellectual pursuit for an answer to the question of our existence. The philosophy of Zen is not that there is no answer, but that there is in fact no question, except as it exists as a bothersome illusion. The enlightening experience of Zen is the elimination of the intellectual question.

In summary, philosophy quiets the intellectual question of our existence by supplying a neutralizing intellectual answer. Zen stills the mind by completely removing the intellectual question.

### The Individual and Society

#### I

When men truly realize the inevitability of their death, they discover the desire for two types of action:

1) to pursue immediate pleasure.
2) to build some monument to themselves that outlives them.

Examining these prospects, we see that great natural disasters, such as floods and earthquakes, cause men to exclaim, "What's the use of building anything when in a matter of time it is sure to be destroyed." Such an attitude—such a belief in the meaninglessness of life leads one to declare, "Let us live for the present and enjoy ourselves." However, such zealous pursuit of pleasure leads us to the use of ecstasy-producing drugs or other excesses which result in physical damage and death. Such death is itself insignificant to such a libertine, except that it terminates the possibility of experiencing further pleasure, and of fulfilling the second desire, that of creating some enduring monument to record our "once-upon-a-time" presence on the face of the earth.

To pursue only the building of some monument to our fleeting personalities, and thus ignore altogether the desire for pleasure, is also unsatisfactory. For everyone realizes that even the pyramids will be reduced to grains of sand in time. So man must also devote some time to a consideration of the future and to creating a better world.

Understand that when I use the word "monument" I am not referring only to such vain edifices as statues, but to all creative endeavors which result in the production of an item whose lifespan is potentially greater than that of the creator; e.g., this writing as compared to me.

To summarize this section, we have seen that man tends towards pursuing pleasure, and towards contributing to something more lasting than himself—civilization. We have also seen that the first men pursued only primal satisfaction of appetites, but that after witnessing many human deaths, a threat was realized to existence and they therefore desired for something permanent in which to take refuge. Thus emerged civilization. Lastly, it has been said that man can be truly happy only when he devotes time to both the experiencing of pleasure and to contributing to the civilization. When a balance between these two factors is achieved, man is truly happy and content. But likewise, when man believes he is not successful in pursuing one of these goals, he takes refuge in the other, and pursues it to excess. Thus moral degeneration, as witnessed in excess drinking of alcohol, occurs among people who do not feel any satisfaction, nor realize any significance or lasting value in their work.

## II

In creating civilization, man was searching to build something permanent and stable in which to take refuge. Thus, by devoting his life to the betterment and continuation of civilization, man attains immortality. But for those who realize that civilization is not eternal, there seems to be no sanctuary. In desperate pursuit of security and peace, man looks to other humans. But they are just as troubled, and so he realizes that they too are transient and passing. He places his hopes in the pursuit of absolute pleasure and ecstasy, only to find that it is not absolute and must be sought again and again in vain. Truly the answer lies in realization of the True Self, and thus the blissful awareness of the immortality of the soul.

But those who cannot realize that only God is

eternal and worthy of pursuit, should live in moderation, effecting a harmony in their lives between the pursuit of pleasure and the practice of discipline. Pursue pleasure; this needs no explanation or reason. Realize that your work, and all of life's activities such as raising children is God's work, and devote yourself to it. Try your utmost to better civilization, for death will only see you born again and again in the world. As reincarnation is a fact, and death is no escape or end, make this world a better place in which to live. You are destined to live again and again in the world of your own mak ing.

### Transcendental Knowledge

### I

To one who does not understand the nature of infection, the amputation of a limb is a severe and destructive act. Yet to one who has knowledge of gangrene, that same act appears as life-saving and merciful. Thus can true knowledge transcend the (apparent) opposition between severity and mercy.

### II

The actions of one who is enlightened stem from true knowledge which transcends reason. Thus his actions cannot be adequately judged or interpreted correctly by those who possess only reason.

Those who possess only reason may choose

from among three possibilities as regards viewing the actions of an enlightened man: (a) they believe in his enlightenment and the ultimate correctness of his actions, and so resign themselves to his being. (b) they reduce the enlightened one's attainment by viewing it in their own light of gross personality. Thus, they regard the enlightened man as no one special and so interpret or judge his actions as they would the actions of an ordinary person. (c) they intellecutally believe in no absolute reality, leaving to each his own. Thus they might believe in the enlightened one's sincerity and belief in himself, and yet still believe their own egos; that is, they would not resign themselves to the enlightened one's will.

## III

Every force in the universe is complemented by a force opposite to it. Further, it is only through the existence of opposites that any forces are known. Thus, pleasure is only known to those who have known pain, and vice versa.

Every concept in the universe automatically implies its opposite. Light is the absence of darkness, and darkness is the absence of light. It is for this reason that no power can mesmerize a people into believing one set of ideas—for· it is impossible to indoctrinate a person with a set of ideas without at the same time instilling the potential for the manifestation of the opposite set of beliefs. This is why the human condition is always one of conflict.

*The Truths of the Grade of Student*

1) He died without ever knowing who he was.

## The Work of the Grade of Student

### I

The work of the Student consists of extensive reading of the theories and practices of the various systems of attainment. The student should study such systems as Christianity, Islam, Judaism, Buddhism, Hinduism, Zoroastrianism, Taoism, Zen, Yoga, the Egyptian and Greek Mysteries and Magic.

### II

The Student must take care not to read such accounts as the Truth, for the Truth can only be known through individual spiritual experience.

### III

The student must take care to balance his readings, and not to prefer any one system to any other system. For if one is biased towards any system he will naturally pursue this method in his practice, and thus become a fanatic and bigot, rather than an Adept.

### IV

The Student should not begin any practice of the recommendations made by any of the systems of attainment. However, he should begin to analize the system, and note those practices which he feels himself to prefer.

### V

The Grade of Student may last for one year or

for many years depending on one's ability to do exhaustive reading in the many systems of attainment.

## VI

The Student should not proceed in his study and practice of this book and its exercises until he is confident that he has a comprehensive knowledge of the various systems of attainment. The Student need not have an understanding of all the subtleties, intricacies, or technicalities of the various systems, for these questions will be answered by one's later research.

## VII

The more information that is given, the more questions that will arise. So too, the more answers that are given, the more need there is for still greater clarification. Therefore, this book presents a minimum of intellectual information, understanding that all questions can be answered by one's own research and meditation. The book concentrates on providing practices and exercises, for only in this way can one actually realize the Truth.

## II

## THE GRADE OF PROBATIONER

### *Methods of Verifying the Truth of Visions*

Numercial or other cryptic solutions confirm an already known truth. Illustration: A Word[1] is given to one as part of a revelation. Later, after much work, the word is calculated to add to the same numerical value as an already known and trusted word; or a word may later be realized as being anagramatic, or in some other way a clue, to an already accepted word. Example: Abraxas has sometimes been identified with the god Mithras because each cabalistically adds to 365.

As regards the above conditions, it must be stated that the analysis of a newly revealed word is extremely difficult work. If it were otherwise, both the word and its solution are most likely emanations of one's own subconscious mind; rather than being messages from some discarnate praeterhuman intelligence.

---

[1]"word" here means a key thought of a philosophy; such as the word "will" to Magick.

23

The interpretation of a vision is itself the work which leads to a fulfillment or realization of the vision or word.

The complexity involved in deciphering a message from a praeter-human intelligence is itself what proves the superiority of the discarnate intelligence involved. Understanding the message is a goal in itself. For the work necessary to understand a word or vision is what increases the knowledge of the magician.


## II

Numerous "coincidences" or associations between objects, incidents, and people arise in daily life to confirm the message of the vision.

One on the Path will discover peculiarly appropriate events occurring to him, especially at crucial stages of spiritual development. These experiences will correspond to a particular problem which is interfering with the aspirant's progress, and will often indicate the solution.


## III

One must assume at the beginning of one's spiritual journey that the revelations of the great prophets are generally true. That is, although there are many differences between the various great religions of the world, the teachings of brotherhood, humanitariansim, compassion, humility, etc., are common to them all. Therefore, if one is subject to visions which greatly contradict these basic intellecutal and spiritual themes, he must use all his Will to realize the invalidity of his visions and refrain from acting upon them.

These three basic methods of separating subjective hallucinations from true spiritual visions were listed in order of descending accuracy. The first method, that of numerical verification, is the best method and should be trusted rather than the other two methods. The last method, with a deviation from the teachings of present religions as grounds for disqualification, is the weakest proof; for it may be one's destiny to cause complete upheaval and reversal in the spiritual life of the world. But unless these dissenting visions be supported stringently by Method I (with further support from Method II), one must not believe these delusions and cause harm in the world.

### Metaphysics for the Probationer

### I

The entire Creation is actually countless impressions, all of which stem from the Original Impression or Whim. The Whim is that which fancied God in the Beyond state to want to know Himself. Thus God in the Beyond state was made dual by the Beyond considering itself as the Universal Unconsciousness and the Universal Consciousness. The Universal Unconsciousness wishes to join the Universal Consciousness but it cannot do so until it realizes itself and actually becomes Universal Consciousness. Then, the two likenesses may unite. All the workings of Creation are the activities of the Universal Unconsciousness endeavoring to become the Universal Consciousness.

## II

It is believed by many that consciousness is dependent upon the physical organism for its existence. This is not the case. Consciousness is eternal and is All that is Real. The physical organism, and the physical world perceived by the physical organism, are both creations of Consciousness. Consciousness creates both these conditions in its attempts to become the Universal Consciousness.

There is only one Universal Unconsciousness which is striving to unite with the one and only Universal Consciousness. But in its attempts to become and join the Universal Consciousness, the Universal Unconsciousness has apparently become separated into many consciousnesses. It has not truly separated in any physical sense, for the Universal Unconsciousness is whole and one. But various whims arose when the Universal Unconsciousness was first caused due to the Original Whim.

These various whims were the repeated and different attempts by the Universal Unconsciousness to reunite with the Universal Consciousness. But as each whim occurred it left its impression in the Universal Unconsciousness. Thus the more attempts that were made by the Universal Unconsciousness, the more impressions that were formed. And the more impressions that were formed the farther apart grew the Universal Unconsciousness from the Universal Consciousness, which is impressionless and pure.

Thus with the repeated attempts and consequent impressions, the Universal Unconsciousness descended lower and lower into illusion until it reached the lowest state which is called "stone."

Now "stone" is consciousness which is still attempting to become and rejoin the Universal Consciousness according to different groups of impressions. (In humans, consciousness is complete and some impressions are experienced as ideas. In humans then consciousness is aware of itself attempting to find happiness according to some philosophy of life.)

Each group of impressions has its origin in one of the early whims of the Universal Unconsciousness to become and rejoin the Universal Consciousness. Each group of impressions so based on a whim is what is called an individual consciousness. The individual consciousness created by the first attempt of the Universal Unconsciousness to reunite with the Universal Consciousness was the first to become and unite with the Universal Consciousness. This consciousness is that of the Avatar.

Likewise down the series of attempts by the Universal Unconsciousness to become the Universal Consciousness are the individual consciousnesses which are evolving towards becoming and rejoining the Universal Consciousness.

The "stone" consciousness will undergo various attempts and consequent impressions in trying to reunite with the Universal Consciousness. These attempts and impressions manifest in the physical world in the form of different species of rocks.

There is one species of stone which is similar to stone and is similar to the first plant. This is a transitory stage in the evolution of the consciousness. Through repeated attempts and consequent impressions, the consciousnesses at this stage will manifest finally as plant, as this is closer towards becoming the Universal Consciousness than is stone.

Likewise, through all the stages of evolution, do all consciousnesses pass. The human stage is the highest manifest form towards uniting with Universal Consciousness.

We think of this evolutionary process in stages because we have generalized and thus have formed the notion of classes of beings. That is, stone is thought of as qualitatively different than plant, and plant different from animals, and so on. But each plant, for instance, is at a different stage of development. Thus plants which we call roses are close enough in evolutionary development for us to classify them all as roses, but each rose is at a slightly different stage in evolution. So it is with humans that we consider ourself one species. But each human is at a different stage of evolution towards uniting with the Universal Consciousness.

Humans are fully conscious of themselves, whereas at the other stages of evolution the beings are not. At the human level, a stage is reached where a process of involution begins. In order to realize the Universal Consciousness, all impressions must be annihilated. These impressions constitute karma and are annihilated through the consciousnesses experiencing their opposites. Thus, one phase of a consciousness might have been its attempt to become and unite with the Universal Consciousness by destroying some other human form. These impressions will be neutralized by that consciousness's assuming another human form and experiencing itself being killed.

# III

These impressions constitute what is called karma, and determine what a consciousness will not do in order to advance more toward rejoining the Universal consciousness.

The energy of the Creation, and its manifestation as the life force, is in fact the primal energy of the Universal Unconsciousness. It is the original energy of the Universal Unconsciousness which drives it onwards toward rejoining the Universal Consciousness, and in so driving the Universal Unconsciousness onwards, the Creation was, and is, manifested.

Each human's life force is a part of the primal energy of the Universal Unconsciousness. Each human regardless of what he may believe himself to be doing, is experiencing the life he is experiencing solely for the purpose of advancing towards reuniting with the Universal Consciousness.

Every act and thought of every human, and every other being as well, is created so as to aid the consciousness become fully conscious and reunite with the Universal Consciousness.


# IV

Karma is not a record of an individual's actions which some superior being keeps so as to cause a soul to incarnate in a certain human form in order for one to experience certain conditions. The soul, or group of impressions which causes consciousness to experience itself as being individual and separate, must attempt to become and reunite with the Universal Consciousness. The soul was once one with the Universal Consciousness, and this is its natural condition towards which it naturally flows. This natural flowing towards the Univeral Consciousness is the stream of life.

The energy of the soul drives the soul onward through the evolutionary states until the soul is re-united with the Universal Consciousness. This energy causes the soul to experience, and what specifically is experienced by the soul is determined by that soul's karma. Thus when one is in human form and conscious of this truth, he determines his own future by living so as to create the proper impressions which will bring him closer towards becoming and uniting with the Universal Consciousness.

So that if one kills animals, it is not some superior being who willfully punishes him. It is this impression and the soul's own need to advance towards rejoining the Universal Consciousness which determines that the soul next experience being a shepherd and caring for animals.


V


When and how a human form (as well as other forms) dies is determined by karma. The consciousness which has experienced all it can experience through a certain human form, and yet is driven by karma to experience further, must assume a new human form. Thus a human form dies, and the consciousness creates a new human form and life in order to experience opposites, and thus annihilate some impressions which are interfering with the soul's uniting with the Universal Consciousness.

## VI

Many believe that the soul, or essence, which is reincarnated is a physical entity, like a bean. They picture that upon death this bean is separated from the body, and that reincarnation consists of this bean being placed into another body. This is not the way reincarnation should be understood.

Understand yourself to be an individaul conscousness. Now, understand that the physical body, the physical senses, and all that is perceived through these media, are creations of the consciousness. The qualities, or nature, of these creations depends upon the level of consciousness, which in turn depends upon karma. The basic point to be understood here is that all lives and deaths are dreams of an individual consciousness. The physical world is created by the consciousness, therefore, the consciousness is not a physical entity; it is not a bean to be placed in independently existing physical bodies. When the consciousness has evolved to a certain level, it simply dreams a new body and a new physical world into existence.

The new body and the new physical world it dreams into existence is appropriate to the new level of consciousness. These levels are determined by the past levels, which are in fact the past lives. To explain karma further—just as a person can only imagine new things according to what he already knows, a consciousness can only dream a new life according to what it knows due to past lives. Furthermore, the process of dreaming this new life is basically one of dreaming the opposite qualities into existence. Certainly this is the most imaginative process, for it produces qualities most different from the preceding ones. Thus if a consciousness dreams of itself as a person killing another person, it will later dream of itself as a person being killed by another person. Thus through these experiences the consciousness will evolve towards the all-experienced Universal Consciousness.

## VII

The comparison of life to a dream is more than an analogy, for a dream, as well as waking life, is a part of the consciousness's experiencing. Psychologists believe that dreams integrate new knowledge obtained during the waking state. Just so, consciousness integrates all its knowledge of the previous life's experiences in the state of death; that is, the momentary state before the consciousness dreams a new life. Furthermore, just as all characters in a dream are said to represent our own personality, all people and events in our life represent the nature of our consciousness.

### The Truths of the Grade of Probationer

(1) The problem of language as an accurate communicator of experiences can be seen as follows: I have written two different accounts of the same feelings or ideas. A person may now like one of these stories and not at all appreciate the other. This indicates that people would be reacting to the actual language employed rather than to an "objective" experience. Thus, in cases of writing about an emotion or experience, it can be said that the experience is separate from the language used to

express it. Hence the apparent illogic contained in certain accounts of mystical experience.

(2) Reasoning only exists where there is complete understanding; that is, when it is realized that love contains within it hatred, and within hatred there is contained love. Without this complete understanding, there exists only rationalization, that is, explanations of misunderstood emotions.

## The Will of the Magician

One begins the magical life with whatever power of Will he has developed through applying himself to the demands of normal life.

At first, the aspirant will promise himself to meditate each day; and this he will accomplish. But before long, a day arrives when due to special circumstances, the aspirant fails to meditate. This constitutes a breaking of the aspirant's original promise to meditate each day. Such failure to meditate is tolerable at this time, because the aspirant is a beginner. But let him be conscious of his negligence and state, "Due to special circumstances, I postpone today's meditation."

If the aspirant continues in his magical work, he must at some point begin developing his Will by practicing his meditation and other exercises more zealously. He must re-devote himself to his magical work, and occasionally, when he feels strongest, overcome the environment and meditate in spite of external conditions. Each time he is victorious over natural situations, the Will gains in strength. When the aspirant's Will is sufficiently developed that he can override what environmental condi-

tions would otherwise dictate, he may view himself
as a magician. But the work of Magick is not to constantly fight the environment with one's Will, but
rather to alter the environment so as to live more
happily.

In practicing Magick, one increases the power of
the Will by first vowing to do easy things, then
vowing to do more difficult tasks. First one vows to
do those things which he normally does, such as
brushing one's teeth. In these cases, the point of
difference is that the magician is conscious of his
act of Willing. He states aloud, "I Will that I brush
my teeth," then he does so. In the second stage,
the magician vows to accomplish things which were
previously just out of reach. Here the magician must
be quite sure that he can succeed in fulfilling his
vow, as a failure would lessen his confidence. After
several successes at this second stage, the magician
is quite confident and the act of vowing contains
within itself the power to accomplish new tasks. In
the third and final stage, the magician vows to accomplish a goal with knowledge that he must succeed. Here a vow means two things: (1) a statement
of desire of a certain goal, and (2) a knowledge
that this goal must be achieved.

When a magician vows, his power to succeed
comes from a desire for the goal, and also from
the knowledge that should he fail to fulfill his vow,
the magician is stripped of magical rank. To fulfill
the vow becomes more important than the original
desire, because once the magician vows, his entire
career and status is at stake. It is therefore apparent that when a magician vows, he is sure that
what he vows to do is absolutely necessary and

correct. For if a magician vows to satisfy some fleeting desire, the vow remains intact and valid while the emotion which prompted it disappears. Thus the magician would find himself pursuing with all his energy an object he no longer desires, but which nevertheless he must attain.

Promises may be broken, but it is when they are kept that the Will gains in power. Vows can never be altered without the magician suffering a loss in magical status. And when a string of numerous vows have been taken and seen through to successful completion, the magician may consider himself a Master. (In practice, those of the first seven Grades make promises; those of the next three Grades take vows; and those of the last three Grades declare oaths. Normally, the declaration of a magical oath is done by a Master to state his life's work or some great task which will involve considerable time to complete. Whereas an inferior magician should not declare a magical oath, the Master may revert to taking a vow as regards some lesser or immediate task.)

As a Master, the magician has a high regard for his record of continuous successes. Thus, the process by which the magical oath becomes the most powerful force in the magician's life is not only one of increasing confidence, but also one of developing respect and a pride in one's magical career. The more important his magical status is to the magician, the greater the power it lends to fulfilling a magical oath. Finally, the magical oath becomes a power in and of itself, providing the magician with a reservoir of strength. The power of the oath, although it was developed by the magician, becomes almost an external power which is stronger than the magician's original forces.

When a magician is in the process of overcoming a destructive habit, it is his thoughts of the great consequences he will suffer which keeps him from indulging in that habit. For example, the magician in order to break a bad habit, vows to do so. Thus, he places his magical status on the line. Now there is a war. Which is more important, one's magical status or the indulgence into the bad habit? Whether or not the bad habit is broken depends upon whether the magician has a higher regard for his career than for indulging in the habit.

The Master has the highest regard for his career and status. Thus, although he may take a lesser vow, it is virtually impossible that he should fail. In his case, if for any reason, the Master reverts to his bad habit, he is stripped of his privileges. No rationalizations for indulgence in the habit are permitted. Not only is the Master no longer a Master, he is no longer a magician. He may if he wishes begin again the entire process of attainment. But he must realize fully what it means to start again down the Path. He cannot state that he is a downfallen Master and is therefore entitled to quicker admittance through the grades. He cannot ask for any privileges or special considerations. He is in fact below the aspirant who is treading the Path for the first time, for the fact that he reached such magical heights and then failed is a terrible defeat which is difficult to erase. Thus, when a Master vows, he must, as he has even more to lose, be even more sure than the inferior magician that that which he vows to do is of great and lasting importance and benefit.

In concluding, notice that the three words, promise, vow, and oath, were used as having different meanings. People break promises. Magicians take vows to proceed in their work. Masters declare magical oaths to change the world.

### The Work of the Grade of Probationer

### I

The work of the Probationer consists of continuing the intellectual research into the various systems of attainment.

### II

The Probationer will also begin to practice those recommendations which he prefers. He will keep a record of these exercises and their results.

### III

The Probationer will also understand that in addition to those practices which are specifically enumerated, it is always the work of the aspirant to contemplate the truths of his grade. Therefore, as probationer, contemplate the truth, "He died without ever knowing who he was."

# III

# THE GRADE OF NEOPHYTE

## *Western Sammasati*

The major work of the Neophyte is the examination of the conscious and subconscious levels of his psychological self. In order to do this, Magick employs a variation of a Buddhist form of meditation known as sammasati.

In sammasati, the aspirant relives all his actions and ideas of that day. Western sammasati is created by performing this analyzation of one's daily activities and thoughts along the lines of western depth psychology.

Mentioned now are some psychological processes which were chosen because they point directly to observable daily life and are relatively easy to spot in one's self. These processes take place unconsciously, that is, one is not usually aware of the processes taking place in one's self. However, one may utilize knowledge of these processes, and gradually, when correctly applied, this will lead to a basic understanding of one's psychological self.

*Projection*—Projection is the process whereby one unconsciously attributes to others those thoughts and feelings which he himself has. The action of their process allows us to see people accuse others of having violent and aggressive thoughts when it is they themselves, and not the accused people, who harbor such thoughts. In another example, a person may hate another, but rather than admit to himself that he has such terrible feelings, he will believe that the other person hates him.

*Displacement*—Displacement allows one to alter in his mind the cause for various emotions. Thus a person whose conscience is punishing him for some transgression may attribute his anxiety to some other more acceptable cause. As another example, one may displace his anger towards some formidable figure onto a more vulnerable target. Thus a man who is not able to disagree and argue with his employer (perhaps for fear of being fired) may return home and have fights with his wife.

*Reaction Formation*—Reaction formation is the name given to that process whereby attitudes opposite to the ones we harbor unconsciously are adopted in order to mask our true feelings from our ego, thus preventing emotional pain. Thus, people who cannot accept their violent and aggressive feelings may participate in peace crusades in order to hide from themselves their true feelings. Another example of reaction formation is seen when one acts *overly* polite towards a person in order to hide one's true feelings of hostility.

As stated, these processes are unconscious. That is, in the previous example, one does not realize his hostility towards a person and therefore decides to hide it by being very nice. One simply finds himself behaving complaisantly unaware of the underlying hatred. The reverse can also occur: one may hate another unaware of the underlying love.

*Compensation*—Compensation is behaving so as to make up for some real or fancied deficiency.

One type of compensation is when a person accepts a substitute which is similar to the person's actual goal. Thus, a woman, who for one reason or another, cannot have children of her own may become a school teacher. In such an occupation her desire for motherhood is partially satisfied.

*Rationalization*—By the process known as rationalization, one finds what appears to be a good reason in order to explain some action which is actually motivated by some unacceptable emotion.

A person, therefore, may explain his giving money to charity by stating all the good work it does, when in reality he is giving in order to alleviate some guilt feeling.

At the beginning of each nightly meditation session the aspirant will review his actions of that day. He will analyze his actions, each individually, applying the knowledge of the already mentioned processes and the new psychological information as he acquires it through his further readings. He will relive each relevant action of that day in his mind's eye and will question himself as to why he acted in that manner. One will continue this practice until one is sure he has come to a true understanding of his psychological self.

The aspirant should not dwell upon, nor even consider, irrelevant actions of the day, in the idea that something may be hidden therein. Only those situations which were, and still are at the time of beginning one's meditation, found distressing should be reviewed and analyzed.

### Symbolism and the Discovery of the Archetypes

### I

It is said that objects or conceptions are symbolic of other ideas. This is a partial truth; for the ideas which are considered by this theory to be "original" are themselves symbols. The entire creation known to us through our senses and mind is but a "symbol" of the struggle of the Universal Unconsciousness to become the Universal Consciousness.

It is therefore incorrect to say that there is no such being as Satan; that he is only a personification of the evil in man. The evil in man is again just a symbol of man's struggle to attain Godhood. Since all is symbolic, it is a trick of language to treat the words "evil in men" as more real than the word (idea) "Satan."

These ideas on symbolism are important in Magick where one deals with the mastering of one's mind. For in order to deal effectively with psychological processes, it is best to see them in the mind's eye vividly rather than to regard them in words. Each psychological process is in fact an individual being which must be conquered. Therefore, believe that Satan does exist; that he is not a symbol of the evil in man, but that he *is* the evil in man.

The reason one can deal more effectively with

a demon than with a group of words which define some evil psychological process is as follows:

In regarding thought processes in pictures rather than words, one is concentrating energy into a more definite construction. There is never a problem of using the same words in describing different processes. There is no problem of various connotations when words are avoided. Also, by transforming clumsy groups of words into pictures, one reduces the number of symbols one must manipulate in thinking, making for more direct and orderly thinking.

These ideas give rise to the below diagram:

*Types of Thinking,*   lowest to highest form.

| Lowest | 1. Verbal (talking while thinking) |
| | 2. Sub-verbal (thinking in words as if talking) |
| | 3. Pictorial (manipulating picture symbols) |
| | 4. One Pure Thought (concentration on one picture symbol) |
| Highest | 5. No Thought (Pure Consciousness) |

## II

The becoming of the Higher Self is a wordless phenomenon. I have tried to illustrate this by referring to this one process in various ways (e.g., the realization of Godhood; the discovery of the True Will, etc.). In the previous section, some steps towards the uncovering of the True Will were discussed in Freudian terms. I wish now to look at the same phenomenon from a Jungian angle.

Freud's subconscious consists of forgotten, or represeed, experiences of this life. The subconscious is "contained" in the mind. Magick says that Jung's collective unconscious is contained in the soul; and that it consists of experiences of the soul in previous lives.

All souls started the path of evolution towards Godhood by beginning as stone consciousness; then progressing through the stages of vegetable, various animal, and finally human consciousness.

The subconscious of people is different because in this life each has had different childhood experiences. But as we live now, we have evolved to a stage of spiritual development wherein most souls have experienced the archetypal situations. That is, most souls have lived during ancient times and have attained an integrated knowledge of these times.

Most souls have lived before; as slaves, kings, magicians, princesses, priests, merchants, shepherds, peasants, soldiers, etc. These souls contain impressions (sanskaras) of these past identities and the knowledge of the past interpersonal relationships of these old identities.

When one penetrates and rediscovers the ancient knowledge of the soul through Magick, he uncovers the archetypes as found, for instance, in the Tarot (e.g., The Magician, The Fool, the High Priestess, etc.). In addition to past identities, one realizes the awe and wonder caused by the knowledge of fundamental ideas; such as those of Death, The Sun, The Moon, etc.

It is true, as Jung has said, that people "pro-

ject"[1] these archetypes unto present acquaintan-
ces. Depending upon the soul's past experiences,
a person has the potential of acting as any of the
characters of the Tarot. Thus a person may today
relate to another as a fool to a hierophant.

There is one further interesting point which
stems from this discussion. The rediscovery of one's
past lives was expressed in terms of understanding
the archetypes. The uncovering of this ancient
knowledge is a facet of Magick. But while examining
its past, the soul itself moves forward one step further in spiritual evolution. This step of progress is
rightly termed mysticism; for it concerns the future.
Stated another way, the looking into the past lives
of a soul is a practice of Magick; the looking into the
as yet empty future of a soul is a part of mysticism.

### The Astral World

Apart from the everyday gross world which we
perceive when we are in our gross bodies, are numerous other worlds which can only be perceived
when we are in the body appropriate to them. Just
as our gross body is actually energy of a certain
vibration, these other bodies are energies of different vibrations. By separating the proper vibrations
of energy from our entire being and placing our
consciousness therein, we perceive a world of phantoms, which are similar in nature to the type of energy comprising our body at that time.

The different worlds have been given names,
such as, the astral world, the mental world, the

[1]Unconsciously, archetypes influence people to behave in certain
ways.

magical world, and the alchemical world. The particular world which one perceives depends on the vibratory rate of the energy composing one's body at the time. The bodies which one inhabits in order to view these other worlds consist of energy of a higher and higher vibratory rate. The consciousness which inhabits such subtle bodies is raised until its rate of vibration is in harmony with the subtle body. *One can say that the subtle body of a higher vibratory rate is the creation of the new state of consciousness reached through certain practices.* Similarly, the phantoms which one perceives are seen by a consciousness of a higher state.

The astral world and astral body is the first higher state after the gross body and the gross world. The astral body can be seen by those who are sensitive to the astral world, that is, those whose consciousnesses can attain this state of existence. The astral body can also be seen by some who normally cannot reach this state of existence, but who do so in the presence of another's astral body.

The astral world should not be thought of as some psychological world of the subconscious. For although some say that the consciousness leaves the body at sleep and engages in activities called dreams, it is possible for one to dream he is with someone, and yet not have this other person dream that he is with the first dreamer. That is, person A may dream of person B but that same night person B may not be dreaming of person A. Therefore, we say that the dreamworld is subjective. However, the experiences of people in the astral world quite often correspond with each other. Therefore, we can say that the astral world, although it may or may not be a Reaility, is at least more objective than the dreamworld.

To explore the astral world one does the following.

The magician sits in his meditation posture, preferably the lotus posture. He then closes his eyes and creates through visualization a body such as his own but sitting opposite him and facing him. When this astral body is clearly visualized one transfers his consciousness to the astral body. Now in the astral body, the magician must concentrate on rising vertically upward through the various worlds. As his consciousness, which is energy, thus vibrates at higher rates, the magician will perceive new worlds and obtain knowledge peculiar to these worlds.

This first method involves the use of a great deal of Will. There is, however, another method which is more passive.

The magician, lying on his back, relaxes by taking a few rhythmic breaths.[1] Next, he intones the sound AUMGN (or some other mantra which has the effect of raising one's consciousness) while concentrating on the point which is the center of his head. This area will then vibrate at higher and higher rates and one will soon be aware that he is outside his gross body.

In both cases, the magician should return to his gross body (his normal state of consciousness) by Willing it.

It is rare that one succeeds the first few times

[1]That is, he inhales to the count of seven, holds his breath for the count of seven, then exhales to the count of seven.

of this practice, so let the magician practice regularly for some time without becoming discouraged.

### The Work of the Grade of Neophyte

#### I

The Neophyte will perform sammasati nightly as already explained.

#### II

The Neophyte will also practice exploring the astral world as already explained.

#### III

The Neophyte will continue his intellectual research into the various systems of attainment. At this time, the research should concentrate on the work of the particular grade. Therefore, as a Neophyte, the research should pertain to psychoanalysis, and other systems of psychology, such as the theories of Carl Jung. The Neophyte must especially concern himself with a study of Sigmund Freud's *The Interpretation of Dreams*. He should then work on understanding his psychological self by interpreting his dreams accordingly. To aid him in this, he should keep a notebook in which he will record his dreams immediately upon awakening.

# IV

## THE GRADE OF ZELATOR

### *The Basic Theory Behind Ceremonial Magick*

The cosmos is one complete phenomenon consisting of harmonious interactions between its constituent forces.

Each man is himself a pure natural force. But due to the action of other forces, in varying and unproportional degrees upon the consciousnesses of men, they become unbalanced, and their true identities are veiled from themselves.

Therefore, there exist men who do not realize their cosmic place and unknowingly act in opposition to the other natural forces. They cause minor disharmonies to arise.

Every act, regardless of how trivial it may appear to some, has echoing cosmic consequences. The raising of the arm, for instance, in addition to changing the arm's position in space, sets into motion the surrounding air molecules. These molecules, by colliding with other molecules, cause still more change. This continues ad infinitum.

The energy involved in this act dissipates readily throughout the cosmos. That is, although the raising of an arm when observed restrictively, may seem to be a drastic change, the energy involved diffuses causing only little change in the cosmos. This is due to the enormous number of air molecules, each of which absorb a fraction of the energy originally involved.

Thus we see that the pure natural force, which is man, is weaker than the combination of the other natural forces. In fact, in most cases where training is absent, a man is weaker than most of the single forces alone.

Imagine that a tornado is one of the forces of the cosmos. If a man were to throw himself in the tornado's path, he would alter slightly the course of the tornado. But as forces, the tornado is the more powerful, and so the man's body would be destroyed. Similarly, a man may act in opposition to the greater cosmic forces. He does exert a change on the cosmos, but in doing so he suffers because he is the weaker.

Rather than suffer, man can be happy. He does this by discovering his True Will, which is the pure natural force he is. He then is able to act in harmony with the greater cosmic forces. When he so acts, his actions are supported by the power of the cosmos. He is therefore successful in his endeavors and is happy.

In addition to merely existing harmoniously with the cosmic forces, man, by coupling his Will with Imagination, can alter his environment and so increase his happiness.

We have now arrived at the basic idea of Magick. It is this: We can attract a cosmic force to us by making ourselves suitable receivers, and then through the use of Imagination and Will, detour the force from what would have been its path, and redirect it towards the target of our choice.

Illustration of this principle:

If an object were to be thrown at an individual, he might raise his hand to stop it. The object and its motion represent the cosmic force. The hand represents the individual. If the force exerted by the hand is greater than that of the traveling object, the object is halted. However, we have already stated that in reality the reverse is true; man is the weaker force. Therefore, in our illustration the hand suffers in its almost vain attempt to stop the moving object.

These are the two general conditions. Man tries not to interfere with the natural forces and suffers only slightly or man interferes purposely and suffers greatly. There is, however, the third possibility which is Magick. That is, in our illustration the person can place his hand *behind* the moving object as it approaches and apply a force in the same *general* direction but changing its path slightly. The greater the force the hand is able to apply the greater the change it can effect.

The hand's force is not great enough to stop the speeding object without suffering (above). However, it can get behind the object and thus utilize the object's own energy to help redirect the object (below).

moving object      new path

proposed path

In the illustration above the intelligence and Will of the man had to be used to select and then execute the strength and direction of force at the proper time. The same is true in Magick.

In the example above, a material object, a part of the body under obvious direction of the Will, was used. The force exerted by the Will in the previous illustration was transformed into the motion of the hand. However, in Magick, the Will is used to control the strength and direction of forces composed of subtler substances, and the energy of the Will is transformed into the appropriate forces by the Imagination.

In the previous illustration, the energy of the Will was transformed into a gross force, for we were dealing with a gross material situation. But the forces which we deal with in Magick are more subtle than the atoms which compose the air. They are acted upon directly by the Will, for the Will is of the same subtle nature.

The forces used in Magick are considered by some to be non-existent. They are non-existent in the same way that atoms were non-existent before appropriate instruments provided evidence for their existence. Just as we can even now not be sure that atoms exist, some can believe that magickal forces do not exist. But just as atom bombs work, so Magick works. It is a poor philosophy to assert that until we can detect these forces spoken of by Magick, they do not exist. For undetected and unrecognized forces nevertheless affect your life.

When one does not know what forces are acting upon him, he is helpless and subject to their influence. Contrarily, when one knows the facts concerning such forces, he can determine his destiny in proportion to the degree of his knowledge.


*Asana*


Asana refers to the assumption of various postures. It is the purpose of these exercises to stretch the spine, increase the blood circulation, and massage and tone up the muscles and internal organs. In doing the aforementioned, the practice of asana also relieves tension and aids overall health. These physical benefits aid the whole being and are prerequisites to pranayama and dharana.

The asanas should be practiced regularly, preferably in the morning. One should not have eaten for at least three hours previous to the practice of asanas, for even a little food in the stomach can make these exercises difficult.

*Asana 1*—Sitting on the floor with legs extended, take a deep breath. Then, while exhaling, slowly bend and grab the feet with the hands. While bending forward pull the stomach in. Continue bending slowly, until the forehead is resting on the knees. Retain this posture for as long as possible, until one has progressed to where he can comfortably remain in this pose for ten minutes.

*Asana 2*—Lie on the floor stomach down. Then place both hands, palms down, one hand atop the other, on the floor, under the neck area. From this position, perform a sort of push-up by extending the arms until they are straight. This will raise the upper body and head. While performing this push-up, inhale deeply. Hold this position for several seconds while also holding the breath. Then, slowly lower yourself to the original position while at the same time exhaling. Perform this exercise six times.

In performing this exercise, it is only the upper body and head which are raised; the legs remain on the floor. This bends the spine especially in the small of the back. Also, when the arms are fully extended, and the shoulders completely raised, one should arch the back still more by bending the head back as if to look at the ceiling.

*Asana 3*—Lie on the floor, on the back. Then slowly raise the legs, hips, and trunk until you are in a shoulder stand position. As you raise the legs and trunk, the hands should be placed on the kidney areas so as to prop one up on his elbows. In the final position, the chin should be pressed against the chest, and one should be standing on the shoulders. One should breathe slowly, while retaining this posture for fifteen minutes.

*Asana 4*—Perform the first stage of this asana exactly as you did Asana 3. Then, from the shoulder stand position, slowly bend at the waist so that the legs are extended back over the head. Continue to bend until the toes are resting on the floor. The legs must be kept straight. As one is bending, the arms which were bent so as to support the body in the shoulder stand, should be placed on the floor.

*Asana 5*—Lie on the floor, on the back. Then, bend the legs so that the feet are resting flatly on the floor. Then, place the hands behind the shoulders so that they are resting flatly on the floor with the fingers pointing toward the feet. Now inhale deeply, and raise the body to form an arch by bending the back and extending the arms and legs. Retain this position for several seconds, while holding the breath. Then slowly lower yourself while exhaling. Perform this exercise three times.

### *Pranayama*

Pranayama is the control of prana which is not breath per se, but a subtle energy which exists in air. However, in this stage of practice, pranayama will be regarded as the regulation of breath for aiding dharana. These breathing exercises place the body at rest and quiet the mind.

The following are general rules regarding the practice of pranayama. These rules are basic to all breathing exercises, except where specifically stated otherwise:

(1) Breathing is always through the nose alone. During the performance of breathing exercises and meditation, the mouth is kept closed.

(2) When one begins an inhalation, he pushes the stomach out thus filling the lower part of the lungs first. Then, the inhalation is continued until the chest rises and the upper lungs too are filled. When inhaling, the lungs should be completely filled, but comfortably so.

(3) Kumbhak refers to the cessation of movement of breath in pranayama. Kumbhak may be performed after inhalation in which case it is a retention of breath, or after exhalation, in which case it is a holding of the breath outside the body.

(4) When the exhalation begins one empties the upper lungs first. Then as the exhalation reaches completion, one draws the stomach in, pushing out

the last bit of air from the lungs. When exhaling, the lungs should be completely emptied, but not with so much force that the peace of the pranayama or meditation is disturbed.

(5) In general, the breathing should be performed slowly, with awareness of what one is doing. One should be highly conscious of one's breathing, as this is a prelude to the practice of meditation.

(6) The breathing must be carefully controlled so that one need never exhale violently or gasp for breath.

(7) When inhaling, one must not violently suck the air in with the aid of the muscles surrounding the nostrils. The air should not be felt as entering the nostrils. The action of the lungs draws the air in, and the first place the air is felt should be the back of the mouth.

(8) When breathing is performed to various rhythms, the counting should be done in the mind, not aloud. The counting must be controlled so that it is an independent standard, and not a reflection of one's need to breathe.

(9) Pranayama is performed by one while in the lotus posture, that is, the standard, sitting cross-legged pose. In cases of old age, or physical disabilities, one may sit upright in a chair, providing the spine is kept straight.

Pranayama 1—One inhales to the slow count of four. One holds the breath for the again slow count of six. One exhales to the count of five. Six complete breaths are done in this manner.

In this first practice, one should aim at perfecting the yogic manner of breathing as outlined in the general rules.

Pranayama 2—One inhales to the count of four, but covering the right nostril with the right thumb so that air enters only through the left nostril. One retains the breath for the count of sixteen. One exhales through the right nostril covering the left nostril with the left thumb to the count of eight. This completes one breath. On the next breath, one reverses the procedure by inhaling through the right nostril for the count of four, retaining the breath for the count of sixteen, and exhaling through the left nostril to the count of eight. Six complete breaths of this type should be done.

This practice is based on the ratio of 1:4:2. Accordingly, one should progress to performing this exercise by inhaling to the count of eight, retaining the breath for the count of thirty-two, and exhaling to the count of sixteen.

Pranayama 3—One inhales and exhales very rapidly, twenty times. (This inhaling and exhaling must be done forcibly, by pushing the stomach in and out rapidly. This quick breathing should produce a hissing sound.) Immediately after completing these twenty breaths, one inhales deeply in the normal yogic manner. This breath should be retained as long as is comfortable, keeping in mind that the exhalation afterwards must be done slowly. Then, one exhales in the normal manner. This completes one round of this exercise. Twenty such rounds should be performed.

### Dharana

The Zelator's first task is to master the asanas.

His second task is to become expert in the practice of pranayama. When both these requirements have been fulfilled, the Zelator is to begin the practice of dharana (meditation).

Meditation, as practiced in Magick, is an exercise of the Will and/or the Imagination designed to increase the strength of and/or develop these forces.

In actual practice, meditation requires that you devote, in most cases, one hour or more a day to its performance. However, as a beginner you will do well to begin meditating for shorter periods, and gradually increase their length to the hour or more. One of the most important points to be made in connection with the length of time of one's meditation is this: If when you begin your meditation session you say to yourself that you will meditate for such and such a time, you must fulfill this promise. The fulfilling of this self-imposed obligation is an additional and vital exercise of the Will. Just as an act successfully completed by the Will increases the Will's strength, so an unfulfilled promise decreases the Will's strength. If one's ability to concentrate has been exhausted, it is useless and detrimental to try to force oneself to meditate any further. It is therefore best to fulfill one's promise by merely remaining quiet and in the lotus posture until the time one has set for himself is expired. But under no circumstances should one interrupt his meditation session and give in to his deficiencies.

One should practice meditating at approximately the same time each day. This soon conditions one's mind in such a way that as the time to meditate approaches and one merely sits down to begin, he is immediately placed in the proper mental attitude. However, as your practice proceeds you will find yourself spontaneously desiring to meditate at many different times of the day. When this stage in your practice is reached you should of course follow such impulses.

It is a good idea to shower, or in some other way, cleanse oneself before the day's major meditation session. This relaxes one's body and if understood symbolically as a cleansing of one's mind, places the mind in a proper attitude for meditating.

In beginning the meditation session one should perform a few favored asanas to relax the body. He should next perform a few exercises in pranayama. After the last breathing exercise, although the counting and concentration on breathing has ended, one should continue to breathe deeply and rhythmically, while beginning the meditation.

Meditation 1—One sits quietly, and suspends through complete relaxation, the function of the Will. There follows quick flashes of memory traces of incidents in one's life, objects, emotions, etc. These manifestations stem from the Imagination.

This process is similar to psychoanalysis' free-association except that one does not speak aloud of the things one sees. Also, one should not try to discover and analyze the meaning of any of these images. One simply relaxes and observes the show.

Meditation 2—In explaining this meditation, a pencil will serve as our example of the object of concentration. When you practice, you may use any object.

First, one visualizes a pencil in the mind's eye. Next, instead of attempting to hold the concentration there, one purposely moves to visualizing an associated object, such as an eraser. As soon as the eraser is visualized, one immediately returns to the image of the pencil. As quickly as we have returned to our picture of the pencil, one leaves it to visualize another associated object such as paper. Once more as soon as one visualizes the paper, he returns to seeing the pencil. This process continues for as long a time as possible in the same manner.

This exercise trains the mind to immediately return to the object of meditation after leaving it for only one association. If the mind did not return to the object of meditation, the condition of mind wandering would occur. This would mean that instead of returning to the pencil, the mind would associate from an associated object, such as the paper. Thus, the next object after paper might be paper plates; and from there one might associate to food, and so on. This form of association leads the mind further and further away from its original object of meditation.

Speed in going and coming, to and from the associated object and the original object of meditation, is used in this exercise in order to deprive the mind of the time necessary to consider more indirect and abstract associations.

Meditation 3—This meditation actually consists of four separate exercises. These four exercises are mentioned in order of progressing difficulty, so that one should practice them in the order they are presented.

The first method consists of counting the inhalations and exhalations of one's breathing. That is, one inhales and counts to himself, ''one''; one exhales and that is ''two''; one inhales again and that is "three"; etc. This counting should be continued until the number ten is reached. At that point, one begins counting again for another set of ten.

In practicing this exercise, and the ones to follow, one should not control the breathing to conform to the counting. The breathing should flow naturally, with the counting being conformed to its rhythm.

The second method consists of counting only on the exhalations. That is, one inhales—no count; one exhales and counts to himself, "one"; one inhales—no count; one exhales and counts, "two." One should continue until the number ten is reached, and then begin another set.

The third method consists of counting only on the inhalations. The counting proceeds as above, but conforms to the inhalations, rather than the exhalations. Again, one should continue until the number ten is reached, and then begin another set.

The fourth method consists not of counting one's breaths, but following them. This means that one simply watches his breaths enter and leave. He realizes himself as inhaling and exhaling, and says to himself, "The breath flows in, the breath flows out." He observes his breathing with great awareness, but thinks not of it, or anything else. In this exercise, one continuously observes the breath for the length of the meditation session; there is no counting of sets.

### The Truths of the Grade of Zelator

(1)     There is no me,
         In this blue twilight dream

Yes, I remember how peacefully I lied
In the clear twilight dream
And how peacefully I died
In the cool twilight dream.

(2)    People fear death becasue they think of the stopping of their hearts. People fear death because they think of the stopping of their breathing. People fear death because they think of pain, or of the coldness of the burial ground. But these things do not pertain to death. Death is a peaceful transformation of consciousness.

(3)    People fear thinking of their death because they feel that such thoughts will hasten their death. This is not so, for a consideration of this state of non-consciousness will free one of fear, and improve one's life.

(4)    If when one dies, he thinks of the world, and says, "I wish I were not dying," he will be re-born.

If, when one dies, he concentrates on the Void, and not on his passing, he will be conscious of his re-birth.

If, when one dies, he realizes Vacuum state, he will never again be re-born.

But to be conscious of the Void at death, one must have experienced it during life. Hence the need to become enlightened. And to realize Vacuum state one must have experienced it during life. Hence the need to become enlightened, and to continue to be enlightened.

(5)    A person should not look to another to supply his happiness. He should first find his own happiness, then share it with another.

(6)     Doctors may ease the pain and prolong life, but sooner or later, each must face death alone. Then no one can help. Therefore, realize that the quest for enlightenment is a personal task.

## The Work of the Grade of Zelator

### I

It is the work of the Zelator to master the practice of asana. Let him not rush this task, but rather let him perform these exercises slowly and deliberately.

### II

It is also the work of the Zelator to become expert in the practice of pranayama. In regard to this task, and the one above, let the Zelator do research into further theories and practices of Hatha Yoga.

### III

It is the work of the Zelator to begin the practice of dharana. Let the Zelator proceed gradually in this practice. He should not attempt to perform many meditation exercises per session. Each meditation previously mentioned, including the different methods of meditation 3, should be practiced independently. Each meditation session should be devoted to only one meditation exercisse.

### IV

The Zelator must contemplate the following

question until he is absolutely sure he has discovered the correct answer. This answer must not be an intellectual response which needs to be justified by logical arguments. The answer must transcend reason.

If I give you three birds, then take them back, what do you have left?

# V

## THE GRADE OF PRACTICUS

*Cultivating Purposelessness*

The major work of Magick is the discovery and realization of the True Will. The other studies and practices are preparatory to the discovery, and are techniques later used in the fulfilling of the True Will.

The True Will is the goal or purpose of one's life. It may be viewed as existing in the True or Higher Self, or the innermost self, or the subconscious mind. The previous information will suffice the Practicus. In a later Grade, more will be said concerning the True Will.

The task which the Practicus must perform towards discovering his True Will, consists of divorcing himself from society. This does not mean a permanent divorce, but rather a temporary condition imposed by the Practicus upon himself.

This isolation from society is not necessarily one of physical seclusion, although this may aid one. This practice of Magick has as its purpose the cultivating of non-involvement with society. The major exercise which is thus undertaken is abstention from reading, listening, or in other ways being subjected to, the news of the world's events.

While it is true that by simply walking out on the streets one is subjected to society, these aspects of the world are quite real; for they are experienced first hand. The society you become uninvolved with by ignoring the news media is a fiction, and this is one reason why you must free yourself from it at this time. The news reports affect the mind, filling it with falsities which when acted upon later in the real society of the streets lead one into trouble.

This trouble is not always of the physical type; it can be, and most often is, of the mental variety. These disorders occur because the mind has been bombarded with thoughts of things which must be done to make the world a better place. But at the same time, the mind realizes its powerlessness to effect such changes. From this combination stems the feelings of alienation and anxiety.

Some believe they do have the power to effect such change, but in most cases, this is an illusion of the Imagination. These people have not realized their True Wills, they have simply been convinced intellectually of the necessity to save the world. Such people when they go about trying to effect change, get involved with things they were not meant to, and find themselves in trouble. In order to avert these troubles, one isolates himself from receiving the news of the world's condition, for it is the news media of the world which implants in one's mind the feeling of necessity of action.

For the reasons already stated, the Practicus should not engage in reading novels, seeing movies or television, listening to music, or in other ways utilizing the Imagination. For any truths which such "stories" convey are truths of another's Imagination, and are not helpful to one who is attempting to discover his True Will. You must not allow any commercials or propaganda to influence your actions. You must be careful not to adopt any outside philosophy as your True Will. The True Will exists already; you must discover that which is already within you.

*Charity*

Here is a misapplication of the law of cause and effect: People believe that their status in life is the result of their own work. Therefore, they believe too that the harder they work, the greater will be their status in life. But realize that in most societies, the difficulty of one's work is not correlated with his monetary income. People do not receive according to the amount of work they do. There are those that do little actual work, but because of the nature of that work, receive great rewards. In most cases, the types of work which do reward greatly for little work, are determined by society's priorities. Thus an entertainer may receive more monetary reward than a research scientist.

Those who believe in the principle of cause and effect, may also believe that they exercise control over their lives. In other words, they believe that their experiences are the results of their own actions. They believe that their fate is in their own hands.

Now realize that all that one has, has been granted to one by God. There is nothing which one has earned by his own hard work. Furthermore, since all that one has, has been granted to one by God, one may at any time lose all he has. Therefore, understand that nothing is truly in our possession. From this understanding, exercise charity to those less fortunate.

The greatest possession which God has granted us is life. We may follow any number of recommendations which insure good health, yet at any time we may fall ill. Furthermore, we may prolong the life of our bodies and minds through medicine and psychiatry, yet at any time these two may break down. Being the greatest possession which God has granted us, life is the most difficult from which to part. We even go so far as to state that killing is wrong, but is justified in the case of self-defense. The highest truth is that there is no time wherein killing another is right. However, in manifested existence, it is necessary to eat to remain alive. Thus to preserve our earthly lives, God has granted that we may eat animals and vegetables. But when we do so, let us do reverence to these living beings which become a part of our lives when we ingest them. Therefore realize that the highest truth is that under no circumstance is it justified to kill another human being. Complete realization of this truth, places one at the mercy of the world.

If one has attained to complete realization of "Thou shalt not kill," he is willing to part with his greatest possession, life. Therefore, he also is willing to part with all other subordinate possessions, such as those which provide material comforts. But if one has not attained to complete realization of the highest truth, the next highest truth is to part with one's material possessions willingly when circumstances so request. When one loses something, let him not rush to replace it. When a possession of yours becomes damaged, do not hasten to repair it. Do not buy and accumulate things due to some fleeting desire. Instead, question yourself as to how much you really want an item, then if you truly desire it, buy it. Give freely to all, whatever you may provide.

But if one has not yet realized this second highest truth, let him consider the third highest truth as regards possessions. No one is totally independent, that is, self-sufficient. Many people have aided one to attain whatever it is one owns. It may appear to an individual that he invented certain plans which others only carried out, but everything has been granted by God—without Him there is nothing. Therefore, do not view your successes as the fruits of only your labor. From this truth, proceed to donate a portion of your income to charities on a regular basis. By so doing, you will be the vehicle by which God aids the unfortunate.

Why does not God simply aid the unfortunate people of the world in a supernatural manner? This is another way of stating the age-old question, "Why is there evil and suffering in the world?" Now just as these truths are graded in a hierarchy, consciousnesses are at different levels of evolution. Just as some will realize truths of different levels, consciousnesses are existing at different stages of development. Those of higher levels of consciousness may be said to be gods as compared to those of lower stages of development. There is no conceit or pride in this statement; for those of higher stages of development are responsible to those who are still creating, and/or beginning to work out, karma. The Creation provides everyone with opportunities to advance spiritually.

In a sense, the unfortunate people of the world are responsible for their plight. That is, their circumstances of life have been created by their karma, the actions performed in previous lifetimes. But in a higher sense, there is no responsibility or fault, because the entire Creation is the whim of God. There was no reason, responsibility, or fault involved in manifesting the Creation.

By this same understanding, there is neither free will nor determinism; for all such questions and complications only occurred after differentiations in the One occurred, and these differentiations had no cause. However, this realization is not easily applied to the physical world. Therefore, other considerations aside, it is best for men to view their lives as determined by their karma. But their karma being unknown to them, let them view the circumstances of their life as all being necessary and good. Let men have faith in God.

To summarize, the highest truth is "Thou shalt not kill another for any reason." This realization obligates one to be willing to part with one's life. This truth frees one, for it demands that he place everyone else first before himself. It is complete selflessness. The second highest truth is that one should own as few possessions as possible. The ones he does own he understands to be granted to him by God. Realization of this truth, obligates one to give to anyone all that he may provide. The third highest truth as regards possesion is that one should not regard his success as due to his own hard work. He should understand that everything comes from God. Understanding this, he should give a portion of his income to charities on a regular basis. Thus he will aid those less fortunate than himself.

### The Truths of the Grade of Practicus

(1) Be happy with whatever comes your way.

(2) Look at what you have, and not at what you have not.

(3) We are prisoners of possessions; for when attachment exists, the owner becomes owned.

(4) We can only ask questions, the answers must be given to us.
   The Creation are the questions. The answers is God.

(5) God speaks to us (consciousnesses) through the Creation.
   Our experiences are our lessons, and thus do we learn.

(6) You cannot die, if God wants you to live. You cannot live if God wants you to die. You cannot do anything, save as God wills it.

(7) Asked to explain how it feels to be an echo, the echo cannot answer, but only repeat the question.

(8) Student: My legs hurt when I sit in lotus.

Master: Then don't sit like that.
Student: How then should I sit?
Master: Sit like the Buddha sat.
Student: But the Buddha sat in lotus.
Master (slapping the student): How dare you presume to know how the Buddha sat!

(9) There are great politicians, great artists, great scientists, and great prophets. Is nothing sacred?

(10) Can we psychoanalyze Abraham, Zoroaster, Buddha, Jesus, Mohammed, or Baba?

(11) One should not speak of what is sacred to oneself.

(12) No matter the great extent of knowledge we possess, we are when healthy very fortunate that we have not succumbed to any disease or loss of faculties. And when ill, we must thank God that we are still alive.

(13) There is no "I." There is only the thoughts and feelings themselves.

(14) New people are created according to sets of Karma.
There is no soul which underlies new personalities.
There is no soul which is the underlying substance for rebirths.
The sets of karma exist in Consciousness.

(15) A memory.

(16) There are many who wish to experience Cosmic Consciousness; and yet if a sacred book

were handed to a schoolteacher, it would be returned with all the mistakes pointed out!

(17) By just turning the pages of a newspaper, the world goes on past me.

*Meditation for the Practicus*

### I

This meditation is an exercise in increasing one's level of awareness. One assumes the lotus posture and simply states silently to himself all that happens as regards his body's actions and his mind's thoughts. So that when one first takes the lotus attitude, he says to himself "sitting, sitting," and so on until he notices the next action. It might be, for instance, that he next swallows some saliva which has collected in his mouth. Here, the meditator says silently, "swallowing, swallowing." His mind may then begin to wander so that he states "thinking, thinking," and so returns to the original idea, "sitting, sitting."

This is an excellent form of meditation because there is nothing which can happen which cannot be incorporated into the meditation, thus preserving the concentration. For instance, if one feels a cramp in his leg, he says to himself, "pain, pain" until the pain goes away. If one feels the need to scratch himself, he instead states, "itch, itch," and the itch will gradually diminish.

### II

The Practicus must very carefully consider the following question. He must contemplate it until he is satisfied he has attained the absolutely correct answer. This answer must not be an intellectual answer which needs to be defended by arguments. It must be one simple answer which transcends reason, and the certainty of which is grasped.

Two persons are fighting. You wish to stop this fighting. You may slap once, either one or the other of the fighters. Do you slap fighter A, who started the fight, or do you slap fighter B?

### The Work of the Grade of Practicus

#### I

The Practicus will not speak concerning his study and practice of Magick, nor will he discuss with anyone various ideas or theories concerning occultism. In this regard, he will keep the Silence.

#### II

The Practicus will not subject himself to receiving, in any way, reports of the world's events.

#### III

The Practicus will not read works of fiction, or view movies, plays, or television, or listen to music. Instead, he will turn his mind inward and analyze his thoughts carefully.

#### IV

The Practicus will not use the personal pronoun "I" in speech.

One may avoid using this word "I" by stating "This is good" instead of "I like this." Also, one may say, "This was written (or done) through me," instead of "I wrote (or did) this."

As a simpler version of this practice, one may use one's name instead of "I." Say, "John Doe liked his visit," instead of "I enjoyed my visit."

# VI

## THE GRADE OF PHILOSOPHUS

### *On Freedom*

#### I

Man's greatest desire is for freedom. But as long as a man has fears, he cannot be free. As long as a man fears death, he cannot be free. So until a man experiences his immortality, he cannot be free.

#### II

Man cannot be free as long as he has fears. And as long as a man is attached to material possessions, there is the fear that he may lose these possessions. So as long as a man is attached to material possessions, he cannot be free. For example, coercion can be applied to a man who fears the loss of his possessions, by a society or a power which can take away these possessions.

75

Likewise, as long as a man is attached to material comfort, he is not free. For a society or a power can control his actions by threatening and proceeding to deprive him of his physical comfort.

Thus the only possession of which no one may deprive a man is knowledge—or power of oneself over his mind.

### III

The reason that systems of attainment, such as Yoga, require a person to free himself of his desire for physical comfort and possessions, is that this frees the person from society or any other coercive power. Thus, the yogi being free from all prejudices, may discover truth. And having found truth, there is no silencing its manifestation; for there is no power which can silence the enlightened man, who fears not the loss of his possessions, who fears not the deprivation of physical comfort, who fears not the loss of his life.

### IV

The point which the ascetic systems of attainmen miss is this: a man can enjoy the physical aspects of life without becoming attached to them. By occasionally suffering the loss of treasured possessions, man tends to disbelieve in the happiness afforded by such possessions. He tends to search for a more lasting happiness, one which doesn't depend on any external object.

When man enjoys some physical comfort, he should not take it for granted. He should not believe its attainment to be the result of his own power, except as his power is the gift of God. A man, and his power to attain anything is part of God; so he should regard any personal possessions as a further grace of God.

## V

When gum loses its flavor, it should be spit out. One should not cling to things which of necessity are diminishing.

It is wrong to fear the loss of that which we have. Each thing should be enjoyed when it exists. When it exists no longer, a new phase of life is begun and what was lost will be replaced by something just as good or better.

One should not in vain stubborness persist in trying to restore something which is disintegrating. One should instead abandon the crumbling project, and devote one's energies to a new, positively creative project.

Trust yourself, for it will exist for as long as you have need of any faith.

### The Rite of Annihilation

Everyone lives as though they would never die. Observe that after the death of a controversial figure, his enemies in life feel sorrow, if not guilt. Notice that these past antagonists honor the dead, making light of their former disagreements.

Through Magick we gain a complete realization of our approaching death. This thought of death should not rob one of life's enjoyments; but let it help us to refrain from violent action which leads to irrevocable results.

The activities of life are appreciated more by the aspirant who performs the following practice. For in realizing the end to life, the magician learns to take nothing for granted. He enjoys life itself[1] and is immune to boredom.

0. Let the aspirant assume the attitude of the dead Osiris. (Lying on his back, with hands folded on chest).

1. Let the aspirant next equalize his breathing by inhaling to the count of seven, retaining the breath for the count of one, and exhaling to the count of seven. Let him repeat this cycle twelve times.

2. Next let the aspirant imagine all the ills and accidents which may befall him. Let him consider the possible ways by which death may overtake him. Let the aspirant take care that these thoughts apply always to himself.

3. In connection with 2 above, let the aspirant contemplate the unpredictability and transience of life.

4. Now let the aspirant be killed by one of the possible methods, e.g., poisoning. This he must imagine most vividly and carefully.

5. Let him feel the life leaving him, and the death covering him.

6. Let the aspirant next experience his body undergoing the processes of embalming, etc.

7. Let him also witness his funeral and feel his burial.

---

[1]. . . life itself-existence; life stripped of novel and exciting items.

8. Let the mind cease thought momentarily.

9. Now a sparkling and divine light from above falls upon the aspirant's eyes opening them. The energy expands to cover the aspirant's body and he inhales a revitalizing holy breath. The glorious magician breathes deep and regularly and the senses rewaken to life. The aspirant is dead; and the magician is born into the Life of Magick.

### Meditations for the Philosophus

### I

One takes the sound Aumgn (pronounced Om or Aum) and repeats it aloud over and over, concentrating on the sound of this word. Or one may take the chant "Hare Krishna, Hare Krishna, Hare Krishna, Hare Hare: Hare Rama, Hare Rama, Hare Rama, Hare Hare," and repeat this aloud over and over again.

This form of meditation does not involve thinking upon the meaning of the word Aumgn. It is not the meanings, but the vibrations of these particular sounds which affect the changes in one's being. This meditation should be practiced at regular intervals or whenever one is in need of tranquillity and replenishing one's energies.

### II

One breathes to the ratio of 7:7:7, that is, he inhales to the count of seven, retains this breath for the same count, and exhales also to the count of seven.

Visualize each inhalation as the sound Hum and blue in color. Visualize each retention of breath as the sound Ah and red in color. Visualize each expiration as the sound Aumgn and white in color.

The red Ah is the fire which transforms the blue Hum of neutral energy into the white Aumgn of pure and blessed energy. This good and compassionate white energy is then dispersed throughout the world with each exhalation.

### The Truths of the Grade of Philosophus

(1) The past is not unfinished business. The past is over, and is no longer real.

(2) Hatred is a cycle. It is up to you to break it.

(3) Remember and forgive. Forgive and forget.

(4) There is no one to hate, for no one can be held responsible for their actions.

(5) Thoughts and actions occur, and may do us harm and cause us sorrow, but there is no entity whose fault this is.

(6) The enlightened man is like a powerful wall. The vulgar may run against him with lies, but he is not affected, for he dwells in the Truth. The vulgar may deprive him of physical life; although this they would not do, for they know that he is immortal as the particles which comprise stone. In the end all that can

happen is that the vulgar themselves be turned into bricks and set into the wall.

(7) I would slap neither, but spit on both.

(8) It was not you which caused yourself to think; nor do you control your death.

(9) Something happened, and here I am. Again will something happen, then there will be no I.

(10) Doubts are the friends of faith.

(11) What is this "I" which makes decisions?

(12) One's name is a tag representing all those thought processes given to one by society. Therefore, if one thinks his name is the answer to the question "Who am I?" he is mistaken.

(13) I have resigned myself; I know that I am in God's protection.

(14) That there is anything to do is illusion. To love God is all there is.

(15) The only thing to pray for is that you may become able to truly love God.

(16) My feet burn as I walk upon the hot stone road. I feel the lives of the people who have walked this way before me.

(17) When I see a person limping, I too feel like dragging my leg. And when I see a person who is blind, I imagine what it would be like not to see.

(18) One day while riding my horse, he turned around and said to me, "stop pulling the reins so hard. You're hurting me."

## The Work of the Grade of Philosophus

### I

The Philosophus will practice non-injury to living beings. He will not consciously harm any living being.

### II

The Philosophus will also practice compassion, speaking the truth, and acting rightly. In regard to speaking the truth, the Philosophus must decide if such truth will harm an individual, emotionally or physically. If speaking a truth will harm an individual this truth is best left unsaid.

# VII

## THE GRADE OF DOMINUS LIMINIS

### *Samadhi*

#### I

Personality is the result of one's previous experiences. Therefore, personality is constantly growing as new experiences are acquired. But at any one time, an individual's personality is the sum of his previous experiences and ideas. If one experiences a loss of memory of all past events, he loses his personality.

In Samadhi, the goal of yogic meditation, one experiences a temporary loss of memory, thus personality. It is personality which veils the eternal self from itself. This is because in the human condition the real eternal consciousness associates itself with the human being's personality. The real eternal consciousness, therefore, mistakes the human personality for itself.

Thus what remains when an individual loses his personality is the eternal real consciousness. Through successful meditation, one experiences a

temporary loss of memory, thus personality. The
real consciousness then experiences itself, and in
doing so, the real consciousness realizes its immortality.

## II

Consciousness exists in and of itself: it is not
dependent upon the physical sensations. Contrarily
the physical sensations cannot exist except as consciousness grants them recognition. Consciousness
must choose to notice the physical sensations in
order for them to exist. In meditation, one chooses
not to notice the physical sensations, thus only consciousness (and memories) exist. In Samadhi, even
the memories, the basis for the subjectivity of consciousness do not exist. Thus is the consciousness
temporarily free from impressions (temporarily
not influenced by impressions) and is One with God.

In these lesser Samadhi, the consciousness is
not truly free, but rather the impressions have become so weak as to become hardly noticeable.
Their re-emergence occurs, however, and terminates
the state of Samadhi.

When the consciousness is truly free from all impressions due to their being destroyed through the
interplay of opposites, the state of Samadhi is never
terminated. Thus, one remains united with God.
This is Nirvana, the end of the cycle of births and
deaths.

## III

Personality, consisting of memory, is what me-
diates between the consciousness and the object experienced. In lesser Samadhi, wherein personality is

temporarily extinct, there is no third condition imposed between the consciousness and the object of meditation. There is no space experienced between the object of meditation and consciousness. They are One.

When a person disagrees with a condition or an idea, it is actually that the condition or idea is termed evil or harmful by the memory (due to education or an unpleasant past experience involving it).

Thus, if memory is eliminated, the consciousness will incorporate, and realize as part of itself, all objects and ideas. When memory is temporarily anesthetized, the consciousness "agrees" with all objects and ideas; for there is no basis for its not "agreeing." This is what is meant by transcending reason.

It may seem a paradox that the consciousness can experience both opposites as part of itself. But this is, in fact, the natural condition. It is not so much that the consciousness would state, "I agree with everything, but I also disagree with everything," but rather that the consciousness would state, "everything is." (and at a further stage of development it would state as well, "Nothing is.")

This explains a mystical experience wherein everything is experienced as One. But the mystical experience is terminated by a re-emergence of personality. Still, though, this experience creates its own impression, and one is made more open-minded.

In the everyday world, one does not experience a state of continuous Samadhi. But practically, one may learn to compensate for the influence of one's

memories, thus effecting a state similar to the temporary loss of personality experienced in Samadhi.
If one were to realize and understand his personality, he could be as objective as the degree to which
he knows the influence of his memories.

This realization and understanding of one's
personality is, in fact, an after-effect óf the experience of Samadhi. For while experiencing Samdhi,
the personality is not truly annihilated, but rather
minimized greatly. The termination of Samadhi
is the re-emergence of the personality. But this termination is not abrupt, but gradual. So that the
consciousness realizes and begins to understand the
personality as it experiences the personality re-
forming. There is a point wherein the consciousness has not re-associated itself with the personality.
Here the consciousness can examine the personality
objectively. This examination by the consciousness
is not conducted along the lines of reason, of
course; but "examination" is a word used to express the consciousness' grasping the truth regarding the personality.

As Samadhi is experienced more and more, the
consciousness understands better, and thus grows
in strength as regards the personality. When Samadhi can be experienced at Will, one has the greatest knowledge of the personality one can have
whilst still being associated with the personality.
Likewise, as one gains knowledge of the personality,
it becomes easier and easier to attain Samadhi at
Will. Thus, the momentum created by the practice
of Yoga increases on its own account, and soon is
a power furthering the advancement of consciousness.

## The Truths of the Grade of Dominus Liminis

(1) It is a common delusion among those who show slight interest in mysticism, or pursue half-heartedly to meditate, that they have indeed dissolved the "ego." It has been said that those very mystics who state their "ego-less-ness" are the most conceited. How then does one know when true enlightenment has been attained?

(2) It has been said that when one attains enlightenment, he must surely know it. This is absolutely true. But what is said about those who believe, who in fact "know" they are enlightened, but are not?

If a person believes he is enlightened, and yet finds himself stating, "I want . . ." he is not enlightened. Likewise, if his problems are personal, rather than having other person's problems his concern, he is not enlightened.

When a person is enlightened, he knows that he is doing God's bidding, and he is resigned to whatever incidents his existence bestows upon him.

## The Mind and the Senses

### I

When I say to one, prove to me that you exist, he is dumbfounded. After recovering, he begins to formulate proofs of his existence. But I reject his words.

To prove to another that I exist, I must slap him in the face with my hand. Then he exclaims, "Why did you hit me?" He has admitted my existence and is requesting an explanation of my action.

This illustrates that one's existence can only be proven to another through the medium of the physical senses. One could argue intelligently and forever, and yet another could remain silent and not recognize the first person's existence. But stab a knife into another's arm, and immediately he will recognize your existence.

If physical sensations did not exist, even the above drastic proof of existence would not be possible. This explains why those who use drugs are viewed by others as being egotistical. Drugs which desensitize the physical receptors, cause one to deny the existence of other beings. Thus the drug user becomes involved with the only thing he considers real, his own mind.

If all physical sensations ceased to exist, one's consciousness alone would remain. The creation would be annihilated. This consciousness which alone remains is still in a state of subjectivity because it contains memories which are remnants of past physical sensations. When these memories cease to exist, pure consciousness remains. Thus, in truth, all that exists is consciousness. Everything else which is believed to exist is only due to a modification of consciousness, which in turn is attributable to the manifestations of consciousness, the mind and the senses.

## II

The difference between the states of consciousness called "waking" and "sleeping" lies in the sensitiveness of the physical sensing apparatus of the body. Thus when one's senses inform one with great intensity of the physical world, one is awake and experiencing reality. When thus stimulated for many, many hours, the senses tire, become habituated to stimuli, and so become less and less sensitive to physical reality. Then, sleep restores to the senses their sensitivity.

While sleeping, the senses are recovering and are being replenished with energy; thus they do not very much inform one of the physical environment. When the senses are thus insensitive, the mind supplies its own stimulation by dreaming. Dreaming is nothing more than disordered thinking; and it is disordered because the senses are not functioning and thus not imposing upon one's visions physical order. For example in the condition wherein the senses are sensitive, that is, the waking state, one realizes the hardness and stability of forms in the physical world. Thus thinking while awake corresponds to one's sensations and is thus orderly and stable. But when the senses are insensitive, that is, when one is asleep, one is freed from the normal order of sensations and thus it can appear in dreams that forms readily change into other forms, hard substances such as wood can melt. Likewise, we can fly in dreams, but when awake we recognize the heaviness of our bodies and do not feel like flying.

### III

When the body is numb, the mind is free.

### IV

The mind is fluid and lives in a world of timelessness.

## V

In searching for eternal life, do not let the present one pass by. Forget the past and future, and eternal life exists in every present moment.

### Meditations for the Dominus Liminis

## O

It is very important that the Dominus Liminis choose only one object to be the subject of his meditation. For it often happens that during a meditation, one may become discouraged by his inability to concentrate. He then decides that it might prove helpful to concentrate upon a different object. It is a very bad practice to thus change one's object during a meditation, for this may develop into a habit wherein one believes himself to be willing all changes in the thought stream. This leads one to mistakenly believe himself to be in control of distracting thoughts.

One should also see that he should never try to solve two different problems during the same meditation session. For the mind will dart back and forth between considering both problems, thereby never fully thinking, and resolving either one. Therefore, let the Dominus Liminis decide upon one, and only one, object to be the subject for one meditation session.

## I

One pictures, for instance, a flower in his mind. That is, he sees the flower in the mind's eye. All the details are present—the color, the odor, the stem, the thorns (if any), the petals, etc. Then one speaks to the flower so as to become friends with it. He touches it. He smells its fragrance. He ponders, without going too far off the subject at hand, all that a flower means to him. He may then place his consciousness in the flower and from this viewpoint consider the man sitting there, himself. What must one seem like to the flower? He places his consciousness back to his body and continues his meditation in like manner.

## II

This form of meditation is actually a practice in concentration. One chooses a subject, such as the flower above, and constructs an image of it in his mind's eye. Again all the details are present. These details, may at first be difficult to hold in sight. One should, therefore, add the details one at a time until the picture is complete. That is, you may first see in your mind's eye simply a stem. When this is clearly visualized you color it green and if appropriate add thorns. Next, add the petals, and so on. When the picture is thus completed, one simply holds and observes it for as long as possible. He does not philosophize or form any opinions of the flower as in the previous type of meditation. If it should happen that the image begins to fade, and the mind starts to wander, it may be helpful to change the color, or type of flower. You may, in order to keep the mind concentrated on the flower, cause the image of the flower to spin as if someone had its stem in between their hands and was twirling it. This also would allow you to observe the flower from different angles.

In this form of meditation we want simply to create and retain an image of a flower in the mind's eye. We do not wish to become better acquainted with the flower, as in the previous meditation. One simply observes the flower, and does not otherwise think.

### III

This meditation involves visualizing numbers for the purpose of multiplying or dividing them. One selects two two-digit numbers to, let us say, multiply. Next, he may picture himself at a blackboard or with a piece of paper. He writes the number forty-two, for example, and below it, in the form used for multiplication, the number seventy-eight. He then carries out the multiplication visually the long way, not through any shortcuts. He arrives at an answer. When that meditation session is ended, he should check (through the use of paper and pencil) the answer to be sure that no mistakes were made.

If this exercise would be practiced often, be sure to select new combinations of numbers, the products of which are not already known to you. When you can multiply in your mind's eye two two-digit numbers successfully go on, if you wish, to multiplying two three-digit numbers.

### IV

The Dominus Liminis should practice the form of meditation wherein he places his consciousness in various parts of his body. For example, he should practice placing his consciousness in his hand

and meditating from this viewpoint. He should place his consciousness in his solar plexus and meditate on the perception of the world he obtains from this vantage point.

## V

The Dominus Liminis should cultivate the habit of questioning everything which he senses during his daily activities. He should not believe anything he hears, sees, smells, tastes, or touches.

## VI

The Dominus Liminis should practice that form of meditation wherein he contemplates each part of his body and then dismisses it by stating, "You (that part of the body) are not truly me, for if I lose you I would still be me." In the same manner, the Dominus Liminis should contemplate his emotions and then dismiss them by stating, "I am eternal and never-changing, yet you (the emotion) are fleeting. Therefore, you are not truly me."

## VII

The Dominus Liminis should practice concentrating on the point in the center of his head (approximately in the location of the pineal gland). He should experience his consciousness as a beautiful, small jewel located at this point.

### The Work of the Grade of Dominus Liminis

## I

The Dominus Liminis will practice all forms of

meditation. To this end, he should do further research into the many different meditational practives of the various systems of attainment.

## II

The Dominus Liminis will analyze his senses and perceptions as indicated in the last three meditational practices.

# VIII

# THE GRADE OF ADEPTUS MINOR

## *The True Will*

The True Will is the purpose of one's life. It is the real goal towards which a person should strive during his lifetime. The True Will may be viewed as existing in the True or Higher Self, or the innermost self, or in the subconscious mind.

Each person has a True Will, and it is its discovery which gives meaning to a person's life. Until the True Will is discovered, one is at odds with himself. His energies will be scattered in many directions with the result that few successes will be made in any pursuit. Contrarily, when one has discovered his True Will, his energies are concentrated towards one goal. All his actions have as their ultimate purpose the realization or fulfillment of the True Will. This alignment of one's natural talents produces a powerful being who is confident he will succeed at what is important to himself. In this sense, each relatively healthy person is capable of realizing his potential and becoming a genius.

The True Will of each person may be different. The search for one's True Will is an individual endeavor. No one but the person himself knows his True Will, and only he is capable of discovering his purpose. For this reason, there can be no general formula for discovery of the True Will. However, the entire course in Magick thus far has been preparatory to this task. Also, there are a few general recommendations which will now be stated:

Firstly, one must be more honest with himself than he has ever been in the past. He must strive for the knowledge of his True Will relentlessly, not stopping until he is absolutely sure he has discovered his True Will. To this end, a method of meditation will be suggested.

Secondly, while the discovery of one's True Will is each person's secret, the following will always apply: As one is nearing closer, and in fact is getting glimpses of, the True Will, one will at first resent the True Will. One will become apprehensive as regards the True Will, and one will not at first wish to accept it. It will seem as a stranger, rather than one's innermost self.

One reason for this dislike of the True Will, is that in discovering one's destiny one feels he is losing his free will to choose his own goal. However, the True Will transcends determinism and free will, and identifies both with each other. For the True Will is in fact what one really wants to do, and what one must do in order to be happy and at peace with himself.

### The Principles of Opposites

As one looks around the world, he observes the

play of opposing forces. He does, during the course of his life, experience acts of justice and injustice, freedom and slavery, evil and good. Most seeing such conflicts do not understand the purpose of, nor do they understand how to deal with, such occurrences.

## I

Many people, not understanding the nature of opposites, identify themselves with one side of a struggle or one type of cause. In doing so, they usually fail to realize the necessity of the group or the ideas which they oppose. This leads to conflict among people, rather than to friendships. Liberals, for instance, should realize that their identity depends on the existence of conservatives and vice versa and etc. That is, there would be no light if there were no dark; there would be no up if there were no down. Further, not only does one quality depend for its existence on its opposite, but it automatically affirms the existence of its opposite. Thus, the positive affirms the negative, and the negative affirms the positive. It is impossible to speak of one thing without also speaking of its opposite at the very same time.

## II

There is no purpose (as most would interpret this word) for such opposites. For the existence of opposites arises only in consciousnesses of a certain state. That is, these opposing forces are not of objective reality, but rather, they are of a subjective nature.

These opposites arise in one's mind, for it is a function of the mind to define, categorize, and thus differentiate certain actions and objects from others. It is the mind which receives varying sensations and formulates systems to categorize such sensations. As soon as the mind receives such-and-such a sensation, it classifies it. Let us say it calls the sensation pleasure. It goes on to define the sensation on the basis of another sensation we call pain. Pleasure is the absence of pain; pain is the absence of pleasure. Notice that until one has experienced both sensations he knows neither. For there is no idea of pleasure until one has felt pain.

Through the above process, one comes to know two distinct, apparently opposing, sensations when in actuality there is but one sensation, the sensation of living.

### III

We cast our eyes to the Soviet Union and we see some people who believe in life under communism. We look to the United States of America and we see some people who believe in and live under a republic. We also learn from observing these nations, that they are in conflict; each nation feels that its system is not compatible with the other's system. These nations feel that their ways of life are completely opposite to each other. But all this conflict is reconciled when we realize that all people truly desire is a happier life. It matters not that two people choose to find happiness in differing ways, provided each is content with his happiness and does not try to impose his methods of attaining such happiness on others. We might say, that in the above example, the opposing forces of the ideas of republicanism and communism are transcended and reconciled by the ideal of happiness for each man. In this same manner we arrive at the following truth: God is the One in which all those forces we consider to be opposites and in conflict are transcended and reconciled.

## IV

To illustrate how God the One may appear to us to be the many, an analogy with color photography can be used.

In color photography, the three colors, magenta, cyan and yellow, are used in various proportions to produce all the colors we see in a color photograph. In just such a manner God the One appears to us, due to the nature of our sense faculties, as the many. That is, just as only a few colors lie behind all the colors we see, God the One lies behind all the different things we sense.

## V

If we take three sticks each of different lengths, we can say of the middle one, that it is longer than the first one, and shorter than the last one. Thus, that one stick contains both the quality of shortness and the quality of longness. Just so it is the nature of a human being to have many contrasting qualities. In order to avoid being a hypocrite one should accept his inherent contradictions. You must also accept the contradictions which others exhibit and not accuse them of being hypocrites.

## VI

The middle stick, above, was spoken of as being both short and long, but it could have been said to be neither short nor long.

## VII

Opposites move in cycles just as the light of day follows the darkness of night. To maintain any one quality for any length of time, without regard to the needs of its opposite, is disastrous.

## VIII

We have already said that God is the One in which all opposing forces and conflicts are transcended and reconciled. Now if God knows both good and evil, we, if we would be as little gods, must also know both good and evil, as well as the other forces of the cosmos. Thus there is the statement, through eating and fasting, lechery and chastity, kindness and selfishness, the magician learns to control all natural forces to his ends.

Man has the potential to know the cosmic forces for he contains them all in smaller and varying amounts. He has the potential to control these forces for he has Will. But for man to control certain forces, he must expand his being and unite with the cosmos (the microcosm must join the macrocosm) so that he may, so to speak, work from within. We have already said that man has the potential to do this for he is himself a miniature cosmos (because he contains all the various forces within him). But notice, the cosmos is a harmonious phenomenon. Its constituent forces are in balance.

Most men contain much imbalance of their natural forces. We see people who are all too aggressive or all too meek, all to demoniacal or all to saintly. If we are to lend support from the cosmos we must become like it. That is, we must have knowledge of all the cosmic forces. We must work ourselves to acquire the necessary equilibrium of forces which will let us join the macrocosm.

There is another very important and very practical aspect of this necessity to balance the forces within us. To understand this reason, however, we must first discuss briefly the nature of the spirits we evoke during magical operations.

Many of the circumstances of the operation lend themselves towards producing strange states of mind in the magician. Prior to the operation, the magician sleeps little, eats little, is chaste, prays constantly, burns in his temple mixtures the fumes of which are intoxicating, etc. For this reason, it has often been suggested that the spirits which appear to the magician are nothing but hallucinations.

The hallucination of a spirit, since it would not be seen to exist by most, is not considered a Reality. Yet, the spirit is real. It is real to the person experiencing it and this is what is relevant, for it is he who evoked it and wishes to control it.

To control such a spirit may to some seem like an imaginary struggle. But people's problems are based on imaginary struggles. Are not one's problems based on illusions which the psychiatrist tries to help dissolve? And yet such "imaginary" forces influence people's actions which in turn affect reality. Just as one's erroneous beliefs are a real influential force, so too are spirits true forces with the power to influence.

The spirit is a creation of the mind, but it consists of energy just as does the rest of the universe, and is just as real. The spirit, deriving its existence from psychic energy, is a manifestation of a cosmic force. That is, a spirit used in a magical operation of love, for instance, is a form one creates through Will out of the force of love existing in one's Imagination, the conglomeration of the cosmic forces within one. Thus a spirit used in ceremonies of love, is actually the force of love personified. It is the Imagination which personifies the force and it is the Will which directs the force towards the target.

When a great quantity of energy colored love is directed towards another person in a magical operation, this leaves the force of hatred in one's being unbalanced. This is the great danger of magial operations. For this force of hatred, now manifesting unchecked by the force of love, and not directed by the Will away from the magician, can destroy the magician's sanity if it is allowed to exist unbeknown to him. This is why the magician must know all the forces of the cosmos.

A magician in magical operations, just as an average person in average actions, if working ignorant of certain forces within him is doomed. Psychoanalysis tries to help individuals by uncovering and making known to the individual, thought processes he never knew existed.

Here then is one reason for the magician's careful balancing of his natural forces. His mastership of all his forces depends first on his examination of his being and then the correction of any deficiencies of certain forces. The manner in which this examination and correction of one's being is conducted is our next topic of discussion.

### Reconciling the Opposing Forces of One's Being

The examination of one's being is conducted along the lines of western depth psychology as performed when a Neophyte. Through such analyzation one will come to see the qualities in which he is deficient. The recognition of such deficiencies, even coupled with the knowledge of why such deficiencies came into being, will not in itself always correct this dangerous condition. There are, however, two general practices of Magick which will develop the stunted qualities of one's being. The first method involves rigorous meditation on the qualities lacking in one's being.

If one has, for instance, a fear of reptiles, insects, and other such organisms, he will meditate on the good attributes of such creatures. He will ponder the good aspects of such beings; such as, how they destroy other organisms more harmful to man, etc. He will visualize himself playing among these slimy animal friends, until he reaches a point when such concentration can be maintained for long periods without one's feeling at all squeamish. Remember, these visualizations must be realistic. One must be able to feel and smell, as well as see, the things he's meditating upon. There should be no difference between imagining yourself sitting in the midst of, as in our example, snakes, during meditation and actually being in the presence of these creatures.

Of course, these meditation sessions must come to an end, but the decision to terminate a session should not be influenced by a fear of the Imagination. That is, such a meditation session must be terminated by an act of Will.[1] A condition will be known to be alleviated when one knows he is not ending his meditation due to his not being able to withstand anymore of it.

Notice that by this method one is not actively searching to discover the reason for such fears, or other emotions.[2] He is concentrating on a scene symbolic of an overcoming of such a fear. The repetition of such concentrated thoughts, in time, impresses the subconscious mind to influence and direct one's actions in the desired manner (away from such fears, etc.).

Notice also that this is not a meditation practiced to reach a better understanding of the nature of, as in our example, reptiles. He does not offer equal time to considering both the good and bad qualities of these animals. He meditates to the point of exaggeration on only the qualities he normally does not consider, i.e., the ones he finds revolting and is therefore disinclined to consider.

This then is how one should overcome the imbalance of emotional forces in one's being. There are also difficulties which arise from an imbalance, not of emotions, but of ideas. These unchecked ideas direct one's actions in ways detrimental to one's

---

[1]A good idea is to determine beforehand what will be the length of such a meditation session and force oneself to concentrate on the disagreeable subject until that time has expired.

[2]The psychological reason for such attitudes does, however, sometimes arise in one's mind much to the surprise of the individual.

being and therefore must be counterbalanced by developing their opposites.[1]

The second method by which we balance the forces of our being involves willfully acting in accordance with the qualities one does not yet possess, i.e., acting completely opposite to one's inclinations.

Thus if one sees himself as being too timid let him in his daily life willfully act too aggressive. If one notices he is too modest, let him try boasting at the top of his lungs until this condition of modesty is balanced, etc., etc.

This may at first seem like simple everyday advice, such as telling someone who is afraid of something, "Don't be afraid." But this is not the case; for this is not advice, but a philosophy supported by the practices of Magick. It is difficult, if not impossible, for one to follow such advice as "Don't be afraid" when one is overwhelmed with fear. But through the practices of Magick, one develops the Will to the degree that nothing can prevent him from doing that which must be done. Remember, too, that the meditation on the opposite quality comes before this practice of actually living the picture one has visualized and that this prepares the way.

---

[1]When opposing thought processes are unbalanced, the stronger one has a greater influence on the Will, the force which ultimately determines one's actions. But when two opposing forces are balanced, the Will, not being swayed unproportionately towards any one course of action, can exercise more easily its own power of decision. Thus actions which are Willed are more rational and do not lead one into troubles.

## The Nature of Enlightenment

### I

The young aspirant was walking in the garden, when he spied the Zen Master crying. "Shame on you, Master, for crying in public," he said. "You're supposed to be enlightened and dwelling in bliss." The Zen Master replied, "Stupid, I'm crying because I want to!"

There is no proper way of acting which indicates enlightenment. The attainment is realization of one's True Self. What this True Self is, is unknown, until we become it.

### II

Generally, emotions are thought of as uncontrollable outbursts of energy, anger, passion, sorrow, etc. But as in our illustrative story, emotions can be controlled by the enlightened individual. Emotions do not necessarily disturb the peace of the enlightened individual, but rather, the enlightened individual chooses to express an emotion in order to be afforded the relief of releasing such energy.

The great question involved here is the separation of the intellectual being from the emotional being. We usually judge a person on the basis of his practicing what he preaches. Does an individual act according to the principles he states he believes? As regards the Zen enlightenment, however, this test may not be valid. For the Zen enlightenment is one of personal realization, and does not consist of believing any principles. If a yogi who supposedly practices ahimsa (non-injury to living beings), kills another, we may certainly criticize him. But the Zen Master reacts moment to moment and does what is right only as regards the conditions prevailing in any one moment. There is no general principle which applies to all moments. Thus his actions for any two moments may appear contradictory, but in fact, he is always being true to himself.

## III

I wish now to discuss the nature of the Absolute Truth, and the manner in which one lives in the mundane world of action while knowing the Absolute Truth.

The Absolute Truth transcends all dualities. It is the Whole, The Tao; and it contains within it all the opposites, the yin and yang. This Absolute Truth transcends the normally perceived mundane world. The Tao, or wholeness, of the earth's activities cannot be seen or appreciated except by one who is detached and not affected by the world. Thus the yogis who dwell continuously in the Transcendental realm of existence always perceive the Tao. They are always blissful, and content that everything is as it should be.

In order to discuss the manner in which one lives in the mundane world while knowledgeable of this Absolute Truth, I will use the following illustration.

I have been told by a friend that he is capable of realizing two opposing sides to an argument, but that afterwards, he reverts to one of these sides as his own belief. In other words, he states that he can see equally well two sides of an issue but still believe in only one side as being "true" or "proper." I place the words "true" and "proper" in quotes; I do not know whether he would. In this illustration it is pointed out how one may believe himself to be objective, and yet hold certain beliefs. The individual in this case does not see both sides equally well, for if he did, there would be no basis for always deciding upon the same one side as the truth.

This same individual believes that his beliefs and opinions are the result of his prior experiences. Since I am dealing with Absolute Truth, and not individual reality, how can I allow my individual experiences to be the criterion of truth? How easy it is to have been born under different circumstances, and so experience a different set of truths, and a different reality. Thus, to experience Absolute Truth, we must divorce ourselves of human personality, (and this is what is done in the various systems of attainment). But in order for me to live in the world, I must still remember my personality. Otherwise, I could not experience emotions or desires. So knowing that there is no Truth as regards any mundane incident, I do not make any decisions I do not have to make. Understand, that I do not force myself to refrain from forming judgments. I naturallly do not make judgments unless I must act in a certain case. Thus, since I am not the president of a country, or in fact, the holder of any political power, I have no judgment as regards any wars which occur. I believe in justice according to the Law of Karma. How do we know that it is not right for those soldiers who are killed, to be killed?

Perhaps they murdered people in some previous life-time, and must now experience the nefariousness of the act of killing another living being by having done unto itself what it did unto another. (Of course, the soul netiher kills, nor is killed. Karma is the record, and the soul the registrar, of the acts of the human personality borne out of that soul's previous Karma.) If I did have the power of a political office, I would, if faced with the decision of dictating war or not, pray to God that I would make the right decision and then decide to the best of my ability. I cannot state that it is always wrong to kill, nor can I state that it is always right to kill. Each soul will take responsibility for its actions. However, one may employ his Will to avoid ever having to make such a decision (to kill another). Thus, one may decide never to accept political power.

As regards cases of criminal justice, I am not a judge in one of the criminal courts, nor am I now serving on any jury. Therefore, I feel no need to form any judgments concerning another's guilt or innocence. When I have no power, I state "what will be, will be," knowing that the Law of Karma is infallible and Absolute Justice is always enacted. If I were a judge, and thus destined to be an in-strument of the Law of Karma, I would again pray that I make the correct decision, and then decide to the best of my finite knowledge.

Even when I must make a decision, I feel that whatever I decide is right in the long run. That is, all my actions and decisions contribute to my evo-lution. There is no right or wrong except that we view actions in a limited context. However, knowing

that whatever I will decide will be correct does not
aid me in making my decision. It does, however,
remove the possibility of regret. Since I have decided to live in the mundane world, I have also
destined myself to make decisions which necessarily
cannot reflect the whole Truth. Thus, when forced
to take a stand, I decide a certain argument to the
best of my limited, intellectual knowledge.

### The Truths of the Grade of Adeptus Minor

(1) All such problems of race discrimination, re-
ligious intolerance, and war, are people's diversions
from confronting and overcoming the one real
problem—man's separation from God. It is a vast
fear which keeps people from confronting this im-
ponderable dilemma.

(2) To whom is one indebted for his life, his parents or God?

### Meditations for the Adeptus Minor

#### I

One should cleanse himself and perform asana
and pranayama as he normally does before meditating. Then seated in the lotus posture, one questions himself repeatedly, "What is the nature of my
True Will?" or "What is my True Will?" This
questioning is conducted continuously with a true
and fervent desire for the answer. That is, one must
not repeat this question over and over mechanically.
Each time the question is asked, it is hoped that it
is this repetition of it which will bring the answer.

As one thus questions himself, his Imagination will suggest answers. But all these answers will be rejected by you—for they will take the form of ideas. That is, answers suggested by the Imagination will be such as follows: "Your True Will is to be President,"; "Your True Will is to leave school, or your job, and retire as a hermit," etc. You will recognize the answers suggested by the Imagination because they are suggestions. You will feel yourself formulating such answers. But when the true answer comes, it is no suggestion. It grasps your entire being and shakes it violently. Afterward, a peace which nothing can disturb reigns in your being.

The suggested answers of the Imagination come in words and symbols. Not so with the true answer. The real answer is not an idea or a new theory of yourself. It is not a new philosophy for you to follow. *Through persistent effort in practicing this type of meditation, you become the answer!* That is, this type of meditation alters your state of consciousness. The new state of consciousness you reach through correct practice of this form of meditation is the answer.

This form of meditation should be performed as often as possible. Sitting in the lotus posture, this meditation may last for several hours or more. Also, if this form of meditation is to be the one you practice, you must continually during the day, when it comes to mind, ask yourself, "What is the nature of my True Will?" Further, you might wish, as your practice of this form of meditation is ripening, to devote several days to a week to nothing but eating, eliminating, sleeping, breathing and questioning yourself "What is the nature of my True Will?"

If you would choose this type of meditation, you should know that there is no rest until the answer is found. You should also know that whereas you saw your Will and Imagination increase in strength and develop as your practice of the other forms of meditation proceeded, this form of meditation does not offer such intermediary steps of achievement. There is one objective—to reach the true answer. Any other revelations or realizations although they may later prove useful, should not be dwelt upon and thus become obstacles in the path to the true answer. You must reject all suggestions of the Imagination!

It should also be mentioned that while the Imagination is thus purging itself of its ideas, one may feel anxious, apprehensive, in general, intensely nervous. This is due to the tremendous struggle taking place—the struggle for attaining knowledge of one's True Will. It is not uncommon for intense emotions, crying, and the like, to occur during the practice of this meditation. This is especially the case when one is undertaking an extended meditation session lasting several hours or days. Also, let me say that whereas you must with the other types of meditations be careful not to strain or tense your muscles in the idea that this aids in concentrating, this is especially so in the case of this form of meditation. The violent struggle which occurs during the practice of this form of meditation may lead to muscle tension and headache. Therefore, if you would practice for any length of time, be sure that with each hour of meditation, you stand and walk around your meditation room several times in order to relax your muscles. Do not forget that when you do such walking, and when your meditation session is over, you must still keep in mind the question "What is the nature of my True Will?"

## II

In connection with the above meditation, the magician should practice becoming a new personality each day. That is, he should awake one morning and decide that for that entire day he will play the part of an ascetic and mystic. Therefore, for that day he will not eat or satisfy any other physical desire, but will instead, only meditate. On awakening the next day, the magician should play the part of just the opposite type of personality. He will indulge in any form of behavior he wants to and scoff at spiritualness. The next day, the magician will play the part of a holy person; he will bless all he comes in contact with. The next day, the magician will act very mean and arrogant, and will curse all those he sees.

The magician should perform this practice without regard for what others may think of him. Further, he must not tell anyone of his practice in order to explain his insane actions to others. The magician must learn to accept the abuse of those who do not understand.

Should the magician fail in these practices; that is, should he revert to "his own" personality, he should in some way punish himself in order to reduce the likelihood of his failing again in the future.

## A Matter of Life or Death

Once there was a man named Chang, who one day went with four of his friends to see a film. The film which they saw was reputed to demonstrate great secrets, but was very ambiguous and difficult to understand. Throughout the ride home, the four friends of Chang discussed their interpretations of the film. Chang sat in silence, listening to his companions' search for the meaning of the film. One of them, a man named Ceek, compared the film to a Japanese nō play, for the story preached no morals, but only illustrated existence. Another saw the film to be an examination of the depersonalization of men. Still another interpreted the film to be a warning to the generation, that they must guard against the growing apathy towards violence. The last friend of Chang expressed his feeling that the film was no more than a science fiction story concerning an insane man's existence in a futuristic society. At this very moment, the car in which Chang and his friends were riding was hit head on by a truck, and in one clear instant, all were killed.

Had these companions confronted the film with the same intensity with which they experienced this matter of life or death, the inexplicable would have explained itself.

## The Work of the Grade of Adeptus Minor

### I

The Adeptus Minor will reconcile the opposites

in his being until he has achieved equilibrium. He must not prefer any action to any other action.

## II

The Adeptus Minor will pursue the knowledge of his True Will according to the meditation and practices of this Grade, or according to a method of his own construction.

## IX

## THE GRADE OF ADEPTUS MAJOR

### *The Theory of Ceremony*

The cosmos is one complete phenomenon consisting of harmonious interactions between its constituent forces.

Each man is himself a pure natural force—a True Will.

When one's True Will is discovered, that individual knows his cosmic place. If he continues to realize his True Will (i.e., act as he should) his actions are supported by the strength of the other cosmic forces and he is, therefore, successful in his endeavors.

In addition to merely existing harmoniously with the cosmic forces, man, by coupling his Will with Imagination, can increase his happiness. For we can attract a cosmic force to us by making ourselves suitable receivers, and then through the use of Imagination and Will, detour the force from what would have been its course, and redirect it towards the target of our choice.

The mechanism by which a cosmic force is attracted to us, and then redirected towards the target of our choice, is the Magick ceremony. The theory behind the Magick ceremony is as follows:

Each man is a miniature cosmos; i.e., he contains within himself all the cosmic forces.

The Magick ceremony is the means by which a man, through Will, increases unproportionately[1] in himself the desired cosmic force and then, again through Will, directs it towards what he wishes.

The desired cosmic force is increased by saturating the Imagination, the sum of the natural forces within one, with ideas and symbols representative of the desired force. So that if the desired force be love, the ceremony is based around the conditions for love operations as set forth in the System of Associations. In this instance, the temple would be draped in green trappings, the metal (wherever metal be used) would be copper, the stones would be emerald or jade, the fragrances would be rose or marjoram, etc.

When the desired cosmic force increases by these methods, it eventually reaches a point where it cannot be contained by the magician, the magician finally consumed by the force directs it to the desired target through a final act of Willing.

This last act of Willing is not performed by the magician proper, for he has become the force itself. You will remember that in a Magick cere-

---

[1]Remember that by the time of a major operation, the magician has balanced his natural forces. This phrase means the same as "Harnesses a cosmic force" or "attracts a cosmic force."

mony, the microcosm joins the macrocosm.[2] This is to say that the Mind of the Magician becomes, or is realized, as the Mind of that Universe. More specifically, that special part of one's being which was prepared for the ceremony,[3] now assumes its function as the ruling force in the operation. Thus, the magician is not aware of himself and is not sending a force to a target which appears as something other than himself. But rather, the specially prepared part of one's being becomes the Mind of that Universe and it directs a force within itself, from a magician within itself, to a target within itself.

What is the underlying principle which explains the efficacy of Magick?

First let me say that one cannot be sure of the underlying principle which is the basis for Magick. In truth, it is enough that it works, and that it does so in a ratio which precludes the possibility of coincidence. However, I believe the reason for the efficacy of Magick lies somewhere among the following ideas.

My world is mine, Your world is yours. The World (i.e., Reality) is neither of these; nor has it anything to do with either of these. Furthermore, I make my own world just as you make your own world. I am my world! Things which are in my world (or which are of me) may be duplicated in

[2]This can be experienced in two ways: (1) the macrocosm floods the consciousness of the microcosm or (2) the microcosm expands to fill the macrocosm.

[3]This is the Will of the Operation created during the preparations to the ceremony through the fastings, prayers, purification, etc. See the following essays.

your world (or may also be of you) but the co-incidence of such a duplication does not instill Reality into that duplicated thing. Thus, you and I may both agree we see a building and yet that building is as unreal as if it were seen by only one of us.[4]

I therefore say that anything which the mind can conceive completely and forcefully will occur in what is called the material world.

Even though all we truly know of is Unreality, the magician can, through the use of his Will and Imagination, impose a part of his world on the so-called real world. That is, through the power of Will and Imagination, the magician can cause others to agree upon, or experience, a part of his world, i.e., the magician causes others to duplicate in their worlds certain things which exist in his world.

One method by which the above is done is mass-suggestion created through a major Magick operation. By this process, the magician impresses the most sensitive and most subconscious part of people's minds with a group of thought-processes. These thought-processes, ideas, attitudes, etc., then influence these people to interpret certain of their sensations in the same way as does the magician. That is, these people then perceive a set of sensations in the same way as does the magician. This means that these people have come to experience (duplicate in their worlds), part of the magician's

---

[4]Using here the conventional idea that if only one person saw it, it would be a hallucination, i.e., an unreality.

world.[5] Then, these people, because they think certain of the same things as does the magician, convince others, subtly and conventionally through language, of the reality of this new experience. Thus, a new idea, an event, or a material thing is brought into what is called the world.

## System of Associations

The forces by which the magician works Magick are Will and Imagination. The manner in which these forces, Will and Imagination, are employed will be explained soon. However, let it be understood now that the purpose of the physical aspects of the ceremony is to aid the magician's power of concentration. That is, by becoming physically involved with the operation, as well as mentally, the energy of the magician's entire being is used, thus increasing the probablility of a successful operation.

Since it is the magician's power of concentration which is to be supported by the ceremony, the magician desires all things concerned with that ceremony to be associated with his objective. That is, in order that the magician's Imagination never move to consider anything other than the objective of the

[5]This can be illustrated on a grosser level (but nevertheless a level of Magick) as follows. Let us say I write and have published a novel. This is the work of my Imagination and Will. Let us further say that you acquire a copy of this novel and read it. You are in this manner impressed with certain ideas. If you are positively impressed, that is, if you have identified yourself with my characters and other creations, you may view a part of the world as I do from then on. You have thus been exposed to, and have incorporated into your world, a part of my world. If you are negatively impressed, you have nevertheless been affected by my world, only in a manner different than the above.

operation, all the actions and objects employed in the operation must be relevant to the magician's task. In other words, all the actions and objects employed in the operation must be associated in the magician's Imagination with the desired goal.

To meet this requirement a system of associations is employed. But before explaining how this system is used, let me explain briefly the basis of such a system.

An association, as we shall use the term, is a symbolic relation between two or more things, existing in one's mind. Thus, the color white is associated with, or is symbolic of, good, just as the color black represents evil; the color red arouses in most people ideas of anger, lust, passion, bloodshed, etc., while the color blue signifies peace, tranquillity, harmony, etc.[1]

In this manner, we have in magick the terms Brothers-of-the-Left-hand-Path, signifying those magicians doing evil, and Brothers-of-the-Right-hand-Path, representing those magicians doing good. The use of the word right to represent good in the above terms is due to the fact that the word "right"

---

[1] These associations exist mostly in the minds of people of the western world, i.e., not all such associations are universal. So that, for example, a black American, who has thoroughly analyzed himself and is sure that he truly believes black to be symbolic of the good forces of the world should alter his ceremonies accordingly. See the diagram, Systems of Association to see how the qualities of these colors are employed.

It should, however, be stated that this is a recommendation for aspirants. When the magician acquires sufficient strength, he will employ advanced techniques to purposely objectify his Imagination; that is, bring it into accordance with the traditional correspondences. The advantages of an objective Imagination and the methods by which it is attained, are revealed to the aspirant at the proper time.

also means correct; the word right is found in righteous, etc. The word left, as a direction, may have come to be used to signify evil because the latin word "sinister" means both "left" and "evil," or it may be because left-handed people are in this world a minority and people perhaps like to believe that the forces of evil in this world are also in a minority.

As mentioned in the footnote, the associations used in Magick are not necessarily universal, as was once believed. These associations depend on the magician's individual psychological make-up. So that although the ocean, for example, conveys to most confronted by it, a peaceful mood (perhaps because we all began our lives there, according to evolutionists) this feeling of peace derived from the ocean may not be experienced by a person who at one time almost drowned. However, barring such exceptions, the associations employed by Magick are found to exist in people's minds, regardless of whether they have read or heard of such associations. That is, had you been confronted with the color red before having even read of its associations and had you been asked to describe your feelings about it, you would most probably have answered similarly to the associations I mentioned. This is because such associations have existed in various human activities for many centuries. For example, in marriage ceremonies the bride wears a gown of white to symbolize her purity.

In some cases, it is easy to see how such associations came into being. For example, black, the color of night, the period of sleeping, is associated with death (and therefore other dreaded things) because death was thought to be a state of sleep. Certain other associations also have such natural causes for their existence. As Eliphas Levi has stated, "Superstitions (associations) are instinctive, and all that is instinctive is founded in the very nature of things, to which fact the sceptics of all times have given insufficient attention." However, since we do find in some people exceptions to certain associations, each magician must ascertain through experimentation which associations are best for him to employ in his ceremonies. Therefore, in presenting my system of associations, I offer only a guide based on the rule that all the conditions under which the operation is performed, be representative to the magician of the nature of his operation. If one is performing some operation of an evil nature, he wants to burn a mixture which will fill the temple with vile, evil smelling fumes. In this case I have (in the idea that few people find the odor of sulphur dioxide pleasant) suggested burning a mixture containing sulphur.

The system of associations is used as follows:

Let us say one is performing an operation of vengeance. He sees on the System of Associations diagram, that operations of vengeance are of Mars, that the corresponding number is five, the metal is iron, the color is red (or its derivatives), the perfumes are the gases of tobacco or hemp, and the stone is the ruby. He, therefore, will employ these materials in his ceremony. For example, he will be robed in red, wearing an iron ring in which is set a ruby and standing amidst fumes of tobacco in a temple draped in scarlet and ornamented with

| Planets (gods) | Number | Colors | Metals | Stones |
|---|---|---|---|---|
| Mercury | 1 | Yellow | Quicksilver | Opal<br>Agate |
| Moon | 2 | White | Silver | Pearl<br>Crystal<br>Quartz |
| Saturn | 3 | Black | Lead | Star Sapphire,<br>Onyx |
| Jupiter | 4 | Blue | Tin | Amethyst<br>Sapphire<br>Carnelian |
| Mars | 5 | Red | Iron | Ruby |
| Sun | 6 | Orange | Gold | Topaz<br>Yellow<br>Diamond |
| Venus | 7 | Green | Copper | Emerald |

# ASSOCIATIONS

| Odors | Sign | Purpose |
|---|---|---|
| Palm, Orchid, Lily, Ambergris | ☿ | To obtain knowledge<br>To discover the future<br>To steal or decrease |
| Hazel, Almond Jasmine, Ginseng | ☽ | To raise the spirits of the dead<br>To reconcile love<br>To induce visions<br>To become invisible |
| Myrrh Civet | ♄ | To cause death, destruction or injury<br>To obtain knowledge, especially by calling on the spirits of hell |
| Cedar Oak Poplar Musk | ♃ | To gain wealth or position<br>To gain health and friendship<br>To become invisible |
| Tobacco Cactus Hemp Sulphur | ♂ | To kill, destroy, or cause hatred<br>To cause unhappiness<br>To raise the spirits of dead soldiers, or anything to do with war |
| Sunflower Heliotrope Olibanum | ☉ | To gain money or treasure<br>To gain harmony and friendship<br>To gain the support of powerful people |
| Rose, Myrtle Red Sandal Aloe | ♀ | To cause love<br>To obtain pleasure<br>To gain friendship |

five pentagrams (the pentagram being the five-pointed star).

For operations of dealing out punishment or for other reasons causing misfortune, one wears vestments of black, bangles of lead and star sapphires, and operates in a temple decorated with three groups of three black candles each and smelling of the fumes of storax, sulphur, or civet.

For operations concerned with obtaining knowledge of future events, or some bit of information which can be obtained by no other means, one would be clothed in a pale yellow robe, wearing a ring of some metal alloy upon which rests an opal, and surrounded by the fragrance of ambergris.[1]

These then are some examples of how the System of Associations is employed. Remember that the construction of a ceremony is the work of each individual magician. The important point to keep in mind is that each and every act of the ceremony be relevant to the work at hand.[2]

### The Preparation of the Magician

The magician is prepared for the Magick ceremony by first being purified and then being consecrated.

The period of purification is three days, seven

---

[1]In time, recourse to physical props will be unnecessary. One will simply picture in his mind's eye all the actions and words of a ceremony. However, this cannot be accomplished until an abnormal degree of concentration can be achieved.

[2]Further rules and suggestions are given in following essays. Also, one should refer to the Grimoires for descriptions of the spirits to be summoned.

days, the product of these (twenty-one days), or a multiple of the product (such as forty-two days, sixty-three days, etc.). The length of the period of purification should be decided upon by the magician before he begins this period. In determining the length of this stage of the operation, the magician should take into consideration his mental and physical condition. That is, he should examine the present state of his being and then decide upon the amount of time which will be necessary for transforming his being into the new self created for the operation. If at the end of the appropriated time, one is not satisfied that the transformation is complete, he may extend this period, but he must do so within the first rule cited above.

The purification of one's being is accomplished by the following methods.

First, one isolates himself from his normal everyday world. He abandons temporarily all social responsibilities and retires to whatever will be his place of working. From this point to the end of the operation, the magician remains secluded.

Second, the magician imposes certain regulations upon himself which will remain in effect until the time of the ceremony. The first of these rules has already been effected provided one has isolated himself completely—that is, a vow of silence. The second rule is that the magician remain chaste during this time. The third rule is that the magician eat and sleep sparingly.

Lastly, the magician strictly analyzes his entire being. He examines the causes which led him to decide to perform such an operation. He questions himself as to whether the operation he will perform is necessary and justified. For if the undertaking of such an operation has been decided upon due to some fleeting emotion, the magician will falter as the emotion passes. All operations, if they are to be successful, must be related to the manifesting of the True Will.

If the magician determines that the operation is needed, he next considers what obstacles must be surmounted in order that his operation be successful. He then employs the various practices of Magick to correct any newly discovered faults in his being.[1] Lastly he prays that all those impurities which he has overlooked be washed away.

On arising each day during this stage of preparation, the magician bathes in order to symbolize (and also to aid) the purification which is taking place. After bathing, he dons his robe. The magician if he wishes may don each new day a robe of a purer color in order to symbolize his gradual purification. Thus, he would on the first day of this period of purification don a brown robe. He would on each succeeding day wear a robe of lighter shades until on the day for consecration he is wearing a pale yellow robe. If this period of purification is to be lengthy, it is not practical for the magician to follow this advice. Thus, in the case of such long periods of purification, the magician simply wears each day, until the day for consecration arrives, a robe of gray.

The last day of the period of purification is the day for consecrating oneself. The magician prays

[1]That is, he meditates and acts so as to reconcile any unbalanced forces within his being. These practices should be carried out most intensely and strictly at this time.

for purification this entire day. Then, he takes an additional physical cleansing, and dons the white robe symbolic of the pure new self.[2]

Thus robed in white the magician consecrates himself by annointing his forehead and hands with oil.[3] He annoints his forehead to symbolize that from this point onward all his mental energy will be devoted to the ceremony. He annoints his hands to demonstrate that all his physical acts will be performed in service to the operation. That is, when the magician takes his sleep he declares, "I Will that I sleep in order that I be strong for the work ahead of me." Likewise when he eats, he states, "I Will that I eat in order that I be nourished so as to perform a successful operation," etc.

It is during this stage, that the details of the ceremony are constructed and mastered until the magician knows by heart what he is to do. (However, when rehearsing the ceremony, one should not go so far as uttering the barbarous names nor performing the appropriate gestures). Also, the Magick Instruments are constructed according to the rules which appear in the following essay.

The process of purification has as its purpose the emptying of the magician's mind of all extra-

---

[2]If your ceremony calls for the wearing of a white robe, you may use this same one, but altering it by embroidering the appropriate signs upon it.

[3]This may be olive oil which has first been purified and itself consecrated to its purpose of consecrating. It becomes so, by the (now pure) magician's pronouncing it so. All such prayers, banishings, consecrations, etc., must be sincere and must issue forth from one's whole being. These two requirements fulfilled, the magician may construct his own wording of such prayers, etc. Examples are found in *The Book of Ceremonial Magic* by A.E. Waite.

neous thoughts. It is also the last stage of equili-
brating the forces of the magician's being, thu⌐
assuring that no danger as such imbalance would
allow befalls the magician.

The consecration of the magician is the donning
of all thoughts relevant to the operation. It is the
polarization of all the magician's actions towards
the one purpose of the operation.

In conclusion, it should be mentioned that,
when possible. the different phases of an operation
should be performed in separate rooms. Thus the
process of purification should take place in a room
set aside for that one purpose. When purified, the
magician may then enter the room in which he will
construct the ceremony and its instruments. This
completed, he may enter that room designated as
the Temple in which place the actual ceremony will
be performed.

### The Instruments and Accessories of Magick

In this essay we shall speak of the two most
important magical instruments, the Sword[1] and
the Wand, and also of the magician's attire and the
Magick Circle and its signs.

The first requisite, as stated in the old magical
texts, is that the instruments of Magick be virgin.
That is, they must not have been used by persons
other than the magician and then, must not have
been used for any other purpose but Magick. Also,
the instruments, to be truly virgin, must be made

---

[1]The Knife and Dagger are constructed in the same way.

from materials which are themselves virgin. Instruments which do not meet these requirements are absolutely unacceptable.

This is because instruments which have been employed by others or have been employed for purposes other than Magick, have acquired forces peculiar to those other persons or other purposes. Thus, during a ceremony these liberated alien forces may interfere with the forces one is evoking, causing very hazardous conditions.

It is impractical to furnish all the virgin materials necessary for the construction of the Magick instruments, for this would involve an extremely complicated process. For example, in order to make a truly virgin Sword, one would require iron ore and charcoal. The tools used in digging up this iron ore must themselves be virgin. Thus, these tools would first have to be made from other virgin material. The charcoal could be easily made by burning pieces of wood, but remember to light the wood, not with a store-bought match, but through sparks created by striking flint, or some other acceptable virgin method.

We see that in order to make a truly virgin Sword, one would require a number of virgin materials and these virgin materials can only be obtained by using other virgin materials, a complicated, and as will next be shown, an unnecessary procedure.

If we examine more closely what is meant by the term virgin, as it is used in Magick, we find a solution to this predicament.

We have already stated the reason for not accepting the use of non-virgin instruments—they may contain forces not compatible with the forces to be evoked during the ceremony. Now, understand that the forces which these instruments possess exist in one's mind. Therefore, in order to eliminate these forces and render an instrument virgin, we need only deal with the mind. To explain further, let us suppose one purchases a conversation-piece type of sword in a department store in order to use it in his magical operations. If he were to employ this instrument as is, he would, when he looked at it or thought of it during the ceremony, be reminded of his trip to purchase it, how much it cost, (this operation better work for I've paid a lot of money for this sword!) his conversation with the salesman, etc., etc. Thus, his mind will have broken its concentration on the ceremony, precipitating failure. Therefore, what must be done to render any material virgin is as follows:

Using the Sword as an example, one would take his store-bought sword in hand and assume his meditation posture. He would then, purposely let his mind make all the associations which the sword suggests. That is, he would think of the sword, then of the trip to purchase it; he would think of the sword, then of its cost, etc. In this way, the magician gets the associations out of his system, so to speak. More exactly, he satisfies the need for existence which these associations inherently have. Thus being pleased with having been allowed to express themselves, these associations are willing to be banished from the magician's mind and not appear again for the duration of the operation.

Notice that it is best to at least purchase the instrument new for one's Magick work. An instrument which has been in one's possession for a long time and used often no doubt has many more associations connected with it than one purchased new. Furthermore, not only would the banishing of the associations involve more work, but one could not be sure he has successfully eliminated all the associations, for there may be some existing subconsciously which will arise only under the conditions produced by the ceremony.

After the associations connected with the Sword have been successfully banished, the magician would take the Sword and plunge it into the flames of a fire. This symbolizes, and also supports the idea in the magician's mind, that the associations have been eliminated.

The Sword is then placed atop a structure of the magician's design (a tripod works well) in order to cool. From below this structure, fumes from a burning mixture of cinnamon, myrrh, and galingale should arise and pass around the sword.[2] This fumigation completes the purification of the sword. The sword is now pure and virgin. No thoughts are connected with it, no forces are bound to it. It is inert. In order to be made into the Magick Sword, the sword must be consecrated. This is done as follows. The magician rubs the sword with consecrated oil, pronounces this sword his own and mighty Instrument dedicated to the work of Magick,[3] and wraps the sword in silk of the color appropriate to the nature of the forthcoming ceremony.[4]

---

[2]Any other fragrant and good smelling incense may be used instead.

[3]It is not the words which are said, but the power of concentration and purity of thought which renders the act effective.

In general, the same rules that were followed in the construction of the Sword govern the making of the Wand.

The Wand should be of hazel and nineteen and one-half inches long. The branch from which it is made should be cut from the main shrub with one stroke of the Magick Sword.[5] The branch should be trimmed of its leaves and bark and any knots or outgrowth should be sanded smooth. (Let me remind you that the sandpaper, the sewing materials to be mentioned later, etc. must all be purified and consecrated to their purposes before being used.) Next the branch should be washed in pure distilled water and set atop some structure to dry. Below it, a fragrant smelling incense should be burned. When this is done, the branch is pure, but inert. The magician, therefore, consecrates the branch by rubbing it with consecrated oil until it has absorbed its full, declares it his own all-powerful Magick Wand, and wraps it as before in silk of the appropriate color.

---

[4]The Magick Sword is now the magician's forever more. It is used in all subsequent ceremonies. However, if it is to be used in a ceremony the nature of which is different from the previous ceremony, the Sword must be re-purified and re-consecrated. This becomes easier and easier, as the magician develops greater and greater love for his Instruments.

[5]It is often stated that acts involved with the Magick operation be single. This is because such unhesitated and sure action demonstrates the magician's single-minded determination and lack of ambivalence. He knows what he must do, and does it forthwith. Likewise, in purchasing the materials for an operation, the magician does not argue about the price. If the material is necessary for an operation it must be gotten, without consideration of the difficulties involved in obtaining it.

The robe should be all that is worn[6] and of the color appropriate to the nature of the operation. Upon it should be embroidered the appropriate signs (which will be discussed later) and the names of power employed in the Magick Circle.

In addition to having purified and consecrated the materials and sewing tools, the completed robe should be consecrated to the nature of the operations it is to be used in. Thus, if the operation is of Venus, the robe is green and consecrated specifically to operations of Venus.

It is left to each magician to construct his own Magick Circle. However, I will discuss it and some appropriate geometric symbols briefly.

The Magick circle is generally constructed by drawing two circles, one nine feet in diameter and the other within it, eight feet in diameter. It should be painted upon the floor of the Temple with vermillion, or paint of the appropriate color to which has been added various metalic powders.[7] The magician makes the entire circle, save one gap, through which he will later enter, and after doing so, seal.

Within the space created by the two concentric circles, the names of power are written. Among such names as may be used are Adonai, El, Yah, Elsa, Ehyek, Elohim, Tetragrammaton, Jehovah, Zabahot, Asarchie, Jah, Sachy. The magician

---

[6]Although some magic texts state that hats and shoes be worn, I do not suggest this.

[7]This is the last time I remind you that all your materials, in this case, the paint, etc., must be purified and consecrated.

should investigate the origin of and know why he uses, the names he so employs.[8]

The Magick Circle, just as all other Magick Instruments and accessories, must be constructed thoughtfully and without error. For in truth, the Circle is symbolic of the magician's own aura of protection. The Magick Circle and its names of power are kept in mind, resorted and clung to in order that the magician not be driven wild by the unleashing of his innermost subconscious forces (which are liberated during the ceremony).

The triangle is symbolic of the trinity, as it exists universally (Father, Son, and Holy Chost in Christianity; Brahma, Vishnu, and Shiva in Hinduism; Isis, Osiris, and Horus in the Cult of Osiris; Time, Space and Mind in metaphysics, etc., etc.).

The triangle is drawn outside the Circle, a few feet from it, and has written around it three names of power, one on each side. The Lemegeton states that the three names used in the Triangle of Solomon are Arimematum, Anexhexeton, and Tetragrammaton. It is into the triangle that the Spirit is evoked and remains until he is dismissed.

When viewed, a triangle pointed up symbolizes the good vibrations (such as, the soul, benign spirits, holiness, healing, etc.) while a triangle pointed down represents the evil vibrations (such as evil spirits, black magic, spells, etc.). A triangle pointed down is superimposed over a triangle pointed up

---

[8]This rule is true for all such words, symbols, gestures, etc., employed by the magician. However, this rule is only applicable to those who are intellectually inclined. For those whose consciousness are exalted by the strangeness and mysteriousness of the barbarous names, symbols, actions, etc., this rule does not apply.

in order to form the Double Triangle or the Sign of Solomon.

The Sign of Solomon, because it is formed by the two triangles representative of the cosmos' opposing forces, symbolizes the macrocosm in which all such forces are harmonized. It also has a perfect number of points—six. Six is a perfect number because it equals the sum of its proper divisors excepting six. That is, the proper divisors of six, (one, two and three, add to six). Thus six, and the Sign of Solomon, represent balance, good integration and harmony.

If the Sign of Solomon be placed within the Magick Circle, the magician stands on the left lower point, the bottom point, the right lower point, the right upper point, the left upper point, the center point, and the top point for operations of Mercury, of the Moon, of Venus, of Jupiter, of Mars, of the Sun, and of Saturn, respectively.

The Double Seal of Solomon is formed by placing the Sign of Solomon within a circle and adding names of power. This is a very powerful symbol and should be embroidered on the magician's robe over the chest region, and on satin of the appropriate color to be worn on the forehead and arms.

The tetragram is the four-pointed star formed by crossing two columns. Each point therefore represents one of the four elements (air, water, fire, and earth) and is used in the evocation of the appropriate elementary spirit. The Tetragram also represents the Tetragrammaton—Yod, He, Vau, He.

The Pentagram is the symbol of man; the microcosm (for man with arms and legs outstretched forms a pentagram) and when used in Magick is symbolic of man's power (one point) over the four elements of the universe (the other four points).

Pentagrams may be drawn within the rim of the Magick Circle and outside it. Alternatively, one large pentagram may fill the inside of the Circle in which case one stands on the upward point (symbolizing up and heaven) during ceremonies of good, and on the side of the two points (symbolizing the devil's two horns) during evil ceremonies. Also, one pentagram of pure gold should be set in the Temple's Altar of stone.

### The Oath and Invocation

Taking with him the silken cloth containing all the consecrated instruments, the magician enters the Temple. Once in the Temple, the magician does not leave—so let him remember to bring everything with him the first time.

Next, the magician places all his instruments in their appropriate places on the altar.[1] He then sets about decorating the Temple with the proper drapery and symbols. The last such symbol to be made is the Magick Circle.

When this be completed, the magician enters the Magick Circle through the gap left for him. He enters with the instruments he will use and a brazier of burning coal in which he will burn the appropriate plants and herbs to produce the proper fumes.

---

[1]The exact positions are determined by the individual magician. The rule, however, is that the arrangement appear balanced (to symbolize the balance and harmony in the macrocosm).

The magician then seals the Circle and walks around the inside rim one time in the direction appropriate to the nature of the operation in order to consecrate the Circle.[2]

Now, the first part of the ceremony proper—the Oath.

The magician strikes once on a bell or gong to call to him the attention of the Universe. He then states who he is,[3] and lists his previous magical attainments or works.[4] He next states the causes which led him to undertake the operation and the specific goal or reason for performing the operation. He must explain why the work is necessary to the manifesting of his True Will and, as such, that he must succeed. He swears that he will successfully finish the operation or die.[5]

The magician must then confess before God, Ruler of the Cosmos, all his ugly emotions and ambitious aspirations which led him to dare undertake the operation. This confession must be truthful and sincere and as such should cause the magician to cry and sweat. He begs of God to help him and give him strength to perform the operation successfully.

The magician will hear the answer that the op-

[2]The magician walks deosil (clockwise) in order to consecrate the Circle to good purposes, and widdershims (counter-clockwise) in order to consecrate it to evil purposes.

[3]His magical or True name.

[4]If this be his first ceremony, he tells of the meditations, practices, etc., which he performed in order to prepare him for the ceremony.

[5]This does not mean that he will kill himself if he should fail this particular time. Rather, it means that he will perform this operation repeatedly until he is successful even if it be the only operation performed by him during this lifetime.

eration is of the True Will and must be done. This inflames the magician with his identity and its cause and he feels saturated with energy. He pronounces the oath once more with full knowledge that it can never be undone.

This confession balances the magician's previous declaration, reconciling these two forces. Also, God's assistance is necessary; no operation is successful without Him willing. For God, as Ruler of the Cosmos, is in effect allowing the magician to direct and control a cosmic force normally under His command. Thus, God in a manner of speaking, is temporarily abdicating one of his cosmic powers.[6]

The Oath and Confession completed, the magician again strikes the gong once and lights the proper incense.

The invocation is executed next. There are no rules or agreed upon words for the invocation. It must be a most passionate and sincere prayer stemming from one's whole being. It must be as a meditation, but ending in the entire absorption of the magician's self into the conjured force. Anything which raises the magician's consciousness and drives him into ecstatic frenzy is acceptable.

The uttering of the barbarous names is only one such thing. The magician should recite them

---

[6]It should be understood that this is how it appears to the magician. It may in fact be that God does no such thing; that the magician never exercises any real control over the cosmic force. Rather, it may be that God pities the insane magician for attempting such a feat. Thus, touched by the magician's foolishness (yet still bravery!), God, remaining in control of the cosmic force, grants to the magician that end which he desired.

louder and louder, and higher and higher in pitch, stopping when he feels he will be driven away, and then continuing; until finally, although he Wills that he stop as before, he cannot, and his self is dissolved.

One should not consider the actual purpose of the operation until such unconsciousness of self is reached. Until such ecstasy is attained, the magician should only concentrate on the sounds of the barbarous names. With the uttering of each name, the magician feels his entire being, which is nothing but energy of the purest variety, being raised vertically higher and higher. Finally, he breaks through the skull and heading towards the ceiling of the Temple, looks down and sees the magician still standing in the Magick Circle. Yet the magician's body follows his commands, and words still issue forth from the magician's mouth.

The magician should then call the Spirit into visible appearance. The Spirit should appear in the triangle which was constructed for this purpose outside the Circle. The magician issues his commands while pointing his Sword upward and holding the Wand out in the direction of the Spirit (but having the Wand vertical; not pointing directly to the Spirit) if it is a Spirit called for some good purpose; and pointing the Sword downward and the Wand directly at the Spirit, if it is a Spirit called for some evil purpose.

The words or speech of invocation (constructed by the magician) should be repeated at most three times. If the Spirit does not appear after three such attempts, the magician should be prepared with a second more powerful invocation. This second speech should then be employed in a manner more deliberate and authoritative than the first invocation. If the spirit still does not appear, the magician should threaten the Spirit with curses of the worst and most painful type.

Should the Spirit still not appear, or not comply to the magician's orders, the magician must consider whether it is possible that some other magician or occult group is interfering and trying to turn the force evoked back unto the magician. If this is found to be the case, the magician must pray to God for aid and place a curse upon the hostile persons causing them to desist. The invocations, and if necessary the curses, should be attempted from the beginning again.

If still the force be not evoked, the magician writes the Spirit's name and, if known, the Spirit's sign, on a piece of paper and places it in a black box with vile smelling juices.[7] The Spirit is then ordered one last time to appear (or obey the magician) lest his name and sign (the Spirit itself) will be burned and then buried forever. If the Spirit appears not, the box and its contents are placed in the fire. It may happen that the Spirit will then appear (or obey) in which case the fire should be extinguished immediately.[8]

[7]These things should always be brought into the Circle beforehand in case of just such an emergency. The magician never leaves the circle during the ceremony.

[8]In reality the Spirit is a force of the magician himself. Therefore its not obeying the magician shows it to be dangerous and in need of reprimanding. The curses and threats aimed at the force are really psychological ploys employed by the magician in order to gain control of the force. Therefore, if unsuccessful, the magician must continue to study (but more intensely), his being and correct any faults before again attempting the operation.

Whether the Spirit has appeared or not, the license to depart must be given. This is a precaution taken to prevent the possibility of the Spirit's lying in wait outside the Circle (invisibly), in order to attack the magician when he steps out of the protective boundary.

The magician blesses the Spirit and then orders it to depart. He adds that it should return whenever the Spirit is invoked or called.[9]

The operation complete, the magician should make a detailed record of all that transpired. This should be done immediately after the ceremony lest the memory be tampered with by time.

This record will later serve the magician in ascertaining what truly occurred; for one cannot be objective during the actual ceremony due to the super-normal psychological state existing at the time.

Further, the record will aid the magician in determining the nature of his future operations and indicate new methods to be developed and employed in subsequent ceremonies.

[9]This is the reabsorption of the magician's own force, but it is now, having been evoked and mastered, under the complete control of the magician. Thus, the magician, in addition to effecting a change in some outer region, has further perfected his being. It may well be that the True Magick is worked after such an operation when the magician, thus fortified, re-enters the common world.

# X

## THE GRADE OF ADEPTUS EXEMPTUS

### The True Trick of Taosim

Let us begin with the Taoist illustration of soft water wearing away hard rock. This observation has been used to explain how something soft and yeilding can overcome that which is hard and unyielding. Further, it demonstrates a way by which one may think of soft things as hard things. A reversal is also true—those things normally considered hard are in fact soft.

The above illustration contains a hidden falsehood. It fails to consider the great quantity of water and the vast stretches of time necessary for erosion to occur. However, this oversight does not negate the truths of Taosim, but instead may be used to extend the truths of Taoism so as to accommodate the prejudices of time and space.

Taking the Taoist idea, "everything is equally good," we understand that up is just as good as down; down is just as good as up. Black is just as good as white; white is just as good as black.

Let's consider the bias of space on this truth. If one is transported to a society the majority of whose population are caucasion, he would choose to be white skineed—it's better for him to be white in this case. If one is then deposited in a Negro society, it would be advantageous to be black skinned. We see that under certain territorial conditions, black may be better than white, and vice versa.

Let's now consider time. Imagine that one is trying to follow the Tao, as intellectually understood. There are two things which he can do today. At one o'clock there is a Democratic meeting. Also at one o'clock there is a meeting of the Republican group. Which does he attend—they're equally good?

In the previous demonstration, notice the phrase ". . . the Tao, as intellectually understood." The truly enlightened Taoist would not have even recognized this challenge. He would have thrown the rule of having only two possibilities in my face and done a third altogether different thing.

But even for an enlightened Taoist, what third thing is there which has no equally attractive opposite? The answer is none; and yet every day enligtened Taoists perform action after action. If the opposite inclinations have all been equilibrated in a person, what motivates him to act one way as opposed to its opposite? The answer is "a consideration of time and space."

The enlightened Taoist does not merely exist, or stagnate. He is regularly affected by time and space and therefore acts. But as time and space may change, the enlightened Taoist may create a work of art with his right hand and directly it's finished, destroy it with his left hand. He is bound by nothing and is free from restrictions.

The enlightened Taoist cares no more for one thing than any other thing. He has no opinions of his own. He does not think; he acts spontaneously. His consciousness assumes the shape of its enviornment at any one time. Let's see how this places the enlightened Taoist above the accepted ideas of truth and honesty, and lies and deceit.

On his way home from work, an enlightened Taoist is surrounded by Rightists who will beat him if he answers falsely. "Are you a Leftist?" they ask. The Taoist replies, "No." The Rightists probe further, "Then you agree with us, right?" "Well of course," replies the Taoist; and he continues on his way. But it isn't long before he is confronted by members of a Leftist organization who raise their clubs and say, "We saw you talking to those Rightists, are you one of them?" The enlightened Taosit replies, "No, I'm with you and they almost found out and beat me because of it."

Enlightened Taoists do not lie; nor do they tell the truth. When confronted by the Rightists, the Taoist's consciousness actually assumed the shape of the Rightists' consciousness. He truly was one of them. After being released, while walking in a neutral environment, the Taoist's opposing opinions and desires equilibrated; that is, his mind returned to its usual state of no-mind. Then, surrounded by Leftists, his consciousness was quickly convinced of the correctness of their point of view. The enlightened Taosit's consciousness is like putty in the hands of propagandists.

We should all become enlightened Taoists, and survive. The time has been reached when almost each of us has our own religion or philosophy by which to live. The Wills of almost each of us are strong enough to decide and do things for ourselves. There's no more room in the world for heroes or martyrs. Now, we are each ourselves; and later we will be the same, having converted no one. There is no reason to suffer or die for any cause. The law is spontaneous expediency. The creed is intelligent propriety.

Humanitarianism and brotherhood are the best philosophies, but unfortunately they are impractical and doomed to failure unless everyone, each and every person, subscribes to them. Be assured that such a time of peace will come. But in the meantime the motto is "act intelligently and compassionately towards each being."

If there is a person in the world who would convince, help, and teach each person to love every other person, let him come forth. I would defy him, even if only to maintain the balance of love and hate in the world—the yin and yang, the Tao.

The weak shall inherit the earth was said by a weakling. You must be strong to survive was said by a bully. But this is written for you, each individual reader. It's up to you to discover the path to attainment appropriate to yourself and work towards enlightenment.

Finally, it should be remembered that each sentence in this essay automatically implies its opposite—so there's no need for you to reply with your two cents!

*The Life of the Magician*

Eliphas Levi has said that ''to attain the sanctum regnum, in other words, the knowledge and power of the magi, there are four indispensible conditions—an intellegience illuminated by study, an intrepidity which nothing can check, a will which nothing can break, and a discretion which nothing can corrupt and nothing intoxicate. TO KNOW, TO DARE, TO WILL, TO KEEP SILENCE—such are the four words of the magus inscribed upon the four symbolical forms of the sphinx.''

The magician knows that all men have True Wills which must be fulfilled. The executioner must kill well, just as the victim must die well. This does not mean a resignation to fate; it may be one's True Will to struggle against becoming an executioner or against dying.

The magician knows his own True Will so that he can act according to its demands and thus be happy.

The magician knows that all the apparently opposing forces in the universe are necessary to each other and to him. He recognizes all the forces of the universe and is not biased in the direction of any particular one. He realizes that all the forces are equally important, for each is undeniably itself and therefore one of a kind.

The magician knows and uses both the forces of evil and the forces of good for his own benefit. He is their master; they are his slaves.

The magician knows that such things as grass, flowers, sun and moon are manifestations of natural forces. He loves and enjoys all these natural

forces and their manifestations. (This is not pan-
theism for the magician does not worship these
natural forces, or their manifestations, as God.
Rather, he loves God through loving *all* His creations).

The magician knows that specific Magick ideas
and practices are subordinate to his true purpose.
He knows that to love God is all there is. Therefore,
he knows that the only thing he can truly pray for
is that he may become able to truly love God.

The magician is skeptical of all things. He
knows that nothing is as it seems, and what's worse
is that he acts on this idea.[1]

The magician knows that there is no truth; for
truth is relative.[2]

The magician does not think of good and evil
as absolutes. For although it is said that to steal
is wrong, a man who steals food to feed his starving
family is not committing wrong, etc.

The magician dares to assume the responsibility
of his True Will.

The magician dares to do that which he knows
is right, regardless of what anyone else says or
does about it.

The magician dares to uncover his innermost
subconscious mind and view the terrifying thoughts
living therein.

---

[1] I say this because when the magician first eliminates the founda-
tion for all his beliefs (by asserting their opposites) he feels dizzy. He
has no basis for orientation and feels faint. This open-mindedness, however, soon leads to a sure grasping of Magick. This grasping of
Magick is the understanding of all of life, for Magick encompasses all of
life.

[2] This statement is itself a lie of the most destructive type.

The magician dares to be honest with himself.

The magician dares to study and practice Magick.

The magician dares to do that which it is said cannot be done.

The magician dares to do that which everyone tells him will mean his destruction.

The magician, because he is (due to his knowledge of opposites and other ideas in Magick) the least prejudiced of people, engages in arguments without the least concern over who wins. He is capable of taking any side in any debate.

The magician can argue a point for hours and all along agree with the ideas of the other person.[3]

The magician does not let himself become fixated in any one mood or attitude for any length of time. One moment he is depressed; he appears the victim of natural circumstances. The next moment he is a king, the forces of the universe at his command.

The magician lives from moment to moment in a natural manner. This is not to say that he does not plan ahead and prepare himself for ceremonies, but rather, he does not worry over whether these operations will be successful. (This should not be taken to mean that the magician is unconcerned with, or careless as regards, the outcome of the operation. He simply has no fear of failure.)

---

[3]Magicians often do this simply to frustrate other people and thus teach them the opposite point of view. In this way, the magician helps reconcile the opposing forces in other people's being. Similarly, magicians often make absurd statements and lies simply to teach others to be skeptical.

This last point needs some further explanation. Many people try to lead "perfect" lives. That is, they have certain fixed opinions about themselves which they never even consider altering. These people chart a course for their future and when something occurs which was not listed on their maps they become depressed. These people think of their lives as one straight line leading to one goal and when they are forced to detour from this line they feel they have failed and experience guilt and shame. Contrary to these people, are magicians who work towards their goal but are always ready to adapt to new conditions. Magicians seize upon new circumstances in order to further their progress towards their objective; but they themselves maintain their integrity.

The magician recognizes all his experiences for their purposes. Pain is not bad, pleasure is not good. But pain and pleasure are both experiences which are known. All experiences are part of life and should be realized as purposeful.

Along these same lines, the magician willfully tries to experience as many situations as possible in each lifetime. Also, he purposely tries to balance these experiences; that is, he tries to experience opposite types of conditions.[4]

I will discuss the morals of the magician first, as this discussion will lead into a consideration of secrecy in Magick.

The magician is one who seeks to act in accordance with cosmic laws so that his actions are supported by nature's strength. When the magician does

---

[4]Aleister Crowley climbed the jaggedest and coldest mountains and walked the levelest and hottest deserts.

what he does, and succeeds, he is in accordance with the Law.[5] It follows that those who suffer from changes effected by the magician are not in harmony with the cosmos as is the magician. If these hurt people were in harmony with the cosmos, they could not be very much injured, for the magician can only effect so much change, even on only one cosmic force.

It is similar to the example of the man and the tornado. The tornado has no intelligence, as we think of it. It is simply a specific manifestation of a natural force. It is its nature and purpose to spin turbulently. If a man throws himself in the path of a tornado, it is not the tornado which has decided to inflict punishment; it is the man who has decided to suffer needlessly.

The magician is following his True Will. This is analogous to the tornado's spinning, for both are now doing their proper acts. Thus, should anyone be hurt by any of the changes effected by the magician, it is the injured person's fault; for he is out of his correct cosmic place.

In the above example of the tornado I chose a specific destructive force. It should of course be clear that all the forces are not destructive. There are neither good nor evil forces. A force's designation as either good or evil can only apply to how a force is used in a particular circumstance. Similarly although it may be wrong to lie, it is worse to hurt another living being. Thus, if my telling someone the truth about something will hurt them greatly, it would be best for me to lie.

[5] "Do what thou Wilt shall be the whole of the Law."

Similar to the man in the tornado analogy, is the unfortunate individual who is at that stage where he refuses to believe in the ways of the magician. As one masters his Magick powers, he will notice, more and more, those people who needlessly suffer around him. The magician will also come to learn that these unfortunate people, although they envy the magician's accomplishments, attribute these successes to luck. One cannot condemn these people for they are at that stage where they simply cannot believe in Magick.

Although one cannot blame persons who cannot believe in Magick, and are thus doomed temporarily to suffer, the magician, until he is himself proficient in Magick, must not dissipate his energy in trying to convince or comfort these people. If one wants to believe that the magician's attainments are due to luck, normal materialistic practices, fate, etc., let him. For it is extremely important, to conserve as much of one's energy as possible for magical matters. And the stronger one becomes, the more capable he is of conserving still more energy. This brings me to the matter of secrecy in Magick.

It is true that in past ages, men practiced Magick secretly in order to avoid persecution. However, this should not lead one to think that because today such practices are not illegal, one need not exercise secrecy. For secrecy is a condition necessary to one who is conserving his energies for the purpose of performing Magick.

When one speaks to another of Magick, he uses energy which could better have been used in practicing Magick. Also, when one speaks of Magick, he becomes subject to the attacks of skeptics. The ensuing arguments dissipate the magician's energy. Even if the magician is careful not to let himself be drawn into such an argument, he uses energy in controlling himself thusly. In addition, the statements of skeptics can weaken a magician's confidence in his own powers—a confidence which is of the utmost importance. The aspirant must have confidence that the practices he is performing are efficacious. If he does not have such faith, he will not be able to endure in his practice of Magick for the length of time necessary in order to see results.

The last reason for secrecy in Magick, is that if someone should know what kinds of operations the magician is undertaking, the person may interfere by filling the ether with vibrations opposed to the changes the magician wishes to effect. Absolutely no one must know what operation the magician is performing. Even outward friends may subconsciously oppose the magician's plans and interfere (again through filling the ether with opposing vibrations).

It is for these reasons of secrecy and conserving (and increasing) one's energy that the magician isolates himself during the performance of operations.

*Magick Phenomenon*
*Clairvoyance*

That the brain produces electrical energy has been demonstrated by science. That the mind generates forces which can effect similar forces in the minds of others has been shown by Magick. People who are sensitive to the subtle forces emitted by people's minds can sense the feelings of others.

The phenomenon of sensing the thoughts of a person other than oneself is called *clairvoyance*.

The actual sense receptors of the eyes transform light energy into the energy of the chemical-electrical nerve impulse. It is this nerve impulse which is interpreted by the mind as an image. The subtle forces emitted by the mind need no such transformer. One's mind, if it itself is not producing interfering forces, will be influenced by the generation of subtle forces by the minds of others. Normally one does not sense the thoughts of others, because one's mind is itself engaged in generating many thoughts. In this case, even if one should get a light sensation of someone else's thoughts, the clairvoyant might project his own feelings onto what is actually received, thus distorting the truth of the original thought.

Each mind contributes to the nature of forces which reign in a room, and in the cosmos. Thus, people who have developed their ability of clairvoyance may walk into a roomful of people and feel that happy, or sad, thoughts are being generated by most. Just as a person who is not sensitive may observe with the eyes that people are laughing and infer happiness, the mind of the sensitive person can feel the force of happiness being generated.

One can observe a roomful of laughing people and exclaim, "This place has a happy atmosphere." Or one may dine in a restaurant which has a desirable atmosphere. This expression "atmosphere," refers, in most cases, to the gross psychological effects that an environment has upon the individual. The laughing people may actually be generating quite sad thoughts. For this reason, the mind which is sensitive to the subtle forces of other minds, is capable of determining more accurately than the sense organs the truth of a particular situation.

As mentioned, each mind contributes to the forces which reign in a room, and in the cosmos. But the strength of a contributing force decreases as it is interacted with by other forces. This applies to two forces each emitted by a different mind or division within any one mind.

When one Wills so that his mind is concentrated on one object, that particular force is being emitted. But when not developed, the Will cannot control the Imagination, and thus the mind moves from one thought to the next very rapidly.[1] This moving from one thought to the next, emits many divergent forces which interfere with one and other and decrease the strength of any one of these forces. Also, there is the potential of the Will's strength of force. The intensity of the Will's force is partially due to the quality of the force being controlled. Let us say one is concentrating on an orange and nothing else. This is good. But another mind may be able not only to concentrate on visualizing only an orange, but may smell, taste, touch and hear an orange as well. That is, one's consciousness is completely filled with the qualities of an orange (one's consciousness is an orange) and one's Will can easily direct it accordingly. These last facts should be kept in mind as they will help you to understand much of Magick.

---

[1]This may not be realized unless one is purposely trying to concentrate on only one thing. He then notices many ideas cropping up and calling for his attention.

### *The Power of Invisibility*

In order to understand how the magician may become invisible, we must first understand the true nature of invisibility.

That which does not act as a stimulus, that is, registers no sensation in us, is said to be invisible.

There are two general reasons why a mass may not be sensed by the human organism. Firstly, the mass may be of such a subtle nature, that the gross sense organs are not sensitive enough to detect the mass' presence. Such is the case with radio or television waves. The human organism has not an adequately sensitive receptor to detect their presence. These electromagnetic waves are, therefore, termed invisible. In order to become visible, these waves must first be converted by a radio or television set into the type of energy we are able to sense.

Secondly, the organism's sense receptors are adequately sensitive and do transmit a nerve impulse, but the mind, being occupied with other matters, is oblivious to this impulse and does not translate it into a sensation. The result of this is that the object, although it normally provides a sensation, is now not perceived.

Many discount the possibility of a human becoming temporarily invisible because they are thinking in terms of the first case above. That is, they do not see how a person's material body may be transformed into a matter subtle enough so as not to be detected by others. Although theoretically[1]

---

[1]If one thinks of the body as consisting of tightly packed atoms, which can only be seen when grouped close enough together to form a dense mass, it would be possible to become invisible by separating

this is possible, it is agreed that it cannot be done at this time. However, the magician's invisibility is of the second type.

When about to be arrested by Mussolini's soldiers, Aleister Crowley escaped by becoming invisible. He did this by exercising his Will so that the soldiers were forced to gaze at an object in the other direction. While thus occupied, Crowley was able to walk past them undetected. In this case, Crowley used his concentrated Will to induce non-verbally a state of mass hypnosis. By directing his Will towards the minds of the soldiers, Crowley was able to influence them to become enraptured with an alternative object. An object in the other direction from Crowley was chosen by him in order that his movements shouldn't disturb and free the entranced soldiers.

One will see in himself the feeling the soldiers had if they do the following. When beginning a meditation session, let your eyes remain open. At first you will see those objects in front of you as always. However, continue to meditate. When your meditation is completed you will become aware of the surroundings again. You will at that time realize that while you were deep in meditation, you were not seeing the surroundings. This was because the mind was occupied with concentrating on some other object and therefore did not perceive irrelevant stimuli. Of course the surroundings were still visible to some other person had he been present, and not in such a state of consciousness as you were. This demonstrates what was said before.

these atoms. To become visible again, the atoms would be brought together again and reassembled.

When the Will is adequately powerful there are a number of ways to become invisible. All of these are simply variations on the above general method. The following example is slightly different, but it is mentioned now because although one is not made invisible, it serves the same practical purpose. Instead of causing the soldiers' thinking to become fixated on another object, Crowley could have altered the soldier's perception of himself. Remember, what is seen and what is perceived are different. That which one sees is the pure image free from any associated thoughts. That which one perceives is the image altered, and accompanied by, thoughts. Thus, Crowley, through use of Will, could have altered the perceptions which the soldiers had of him. In this case the soldiers would have seen Crowley, but would no longer have perceived him as one who should be arrested. They would, had Crowley Willed it, perceived him as a friend.

The general method may be employed in order to render an object, other than the magician's body, invisible to other persons. Again, by controlling the people's minds they can be made to overlook an object the magician does not wish them to see. An example of this on the gross material level is that of the expert of legerdemain. Here too, the expert misdirects the audience's attention. Through words and gestures, the magician calls attention to a harmless action, and away from the area where the slight of hand is being exercised.

Another method of making oneself invisible is depicted in the short story, "The Invisible Man." Here it is illustrated that one usually overlooks the ordinary and obvious. In this story, a murder is committed. The murderer in order to have committed his act, had to have entered the building within a certain time period. However, the people in the area saw no one enter the building at this time. In the end justice triumphs, for the investigator remembers a suspect previously overlooked—the postman. Because of his commonplaceness, no one even took notice of his entering the house to deliver the mail.

The true magician is the most well-rounded of persons. This does not mean he is dull and is not at any one time interested in some matters more than others. What it does mean is that his eccentricities are under the control of the Will. Thus at any given time he can call into balance his conflicting processes and become neutral. This neutrality can be displayed outwardly, making the magician appear the most middle-of-the-road, conforming and commonplace of persons. Appearing thusly, he can go his strange way unnoticed and therefore unobstructed.

*Additional Practices*

### I

In the practice of Magick, as in all other matters, there sometimes arise problems. As Magicians, we are concerned with two general types of problems. Firstly, those which involve the magical operation itself—that is, intricacies of the operation which must be worked out. Secondly, those problems which arise from daily living which, and all such problems do, distract our mind and thus interfere indirectly with the magical work.

In the preparation for any magical operation, the being is purified and strengthened. This has been discussed already. I now refer to any one particular problem which may pollute the consciousness and thus interfere with our overall preparation.

In order to rid oneself of any such specific problem the following is done:

(1) The magician assumes the lotus position.
(2) The magician breathes five breaths as follows: First, he inhales to the rhythmic count of eight. Next he retains this breath for the count of twelve; last he exhales to the count of ten.

(3) The magician then places his complete attention to a flickering prayer candle.

Such candles are purchased as Buddhist prayer candles or strobe candles. These candles alternate rapidly between producing light and darkness. The intentful watching of such strobe flames produces a clear mind, very much similar to the nature of the light of the flame itself.

In watching such a candle, one does not meditate, nor even think at all of the problem which first led him to this practice. When one begins this practice, the problem is well known to the magician. It remains in his subconscious mind, where the solution will be formulated. By simply watching the candle and breathing quietly and naturally, with no straining or thought of the problem, the solution will make itself known to the magician.

After the problem has been resolved, the magician will arise and with reverence, put out the candle. But before he does so let him sit awhile longer

in order to make sure the answer received is the
true answer and that it is a full and complete answer.

### *Hymn to the Flickering Candle*

Peaceful, quiet, alone it burns
He who watches it is he who learns
Its flames upward burst and take flight
Passive darkness and healing light
Hidden within the heart of the flame
There lives the truth from whence we came
It's known by us but not in words
By the dancing flame, flight of birds.

Glorious candle burn all night
Giving forth beauty and light
Burn, burn, full and bright
Letting me know all is right
One and off, dark and light
My eyes can't move, you're fixed in sight
My mind lies still, you're fixed in sight
All is peace, you're fixed in sight.

After practicing for some time the attaining of
the passive state of consciousness through the use
of a flickering candle, the aspirant should begin to
practice assuming this state of consciousness without
such aids. This is done as follows.

While attaining the passive state of consciousness through the use of a candle, let the aspirant
observe, without effort, the processes which his mind
undergoes in reaching this passive state. When these
processes are known to the aspirant, let him begin

practicing the conscious control of these processes. That is, let him practice controlling his mind to undergo these processes without the aid of the candle. With practice, the aspirant will be able to willfully attain this passive state of consciousness without the use of any aids whatsoever.

It is this passive state of consciousness which accounts for clairvoyance. By assuming this passive state of consciousness when in the presence of people, one easily becomes impressed with the thoughts of the others around him. To become especially sensitive to any one person in a crowd, one should assume the passive state of consciousness, and then into it put only one thought of this person. This, in effect causes the passive state of consciousness to become slightly more sensitive to the one particular person's mind, in which the magician is interested.

It is a bit difficult to explain this process of clairvoyance. However, as one proceeds in his practice, and develops his powers, he will also develop an understanding of how to use this power; for the knowledge of how to apply this power is inherent in the power itself.

## II

To render one's body (or some other object) invisible, the magician assumes the passive state of consciousness. Then, he Wills one thought picture through this void directly into the minds of the people to whom he wishes to become invisible.

This thought picture, which the magician sends as a beam of light, consists of one, unified, powerful, idea and one colorful, detailed image. The one idea which the magician places in the minds of others, is the idea of the beautifulness of the object with which the magician wishes these people to become enraptured. (Not the idea that the magician is invisible!) The image is a visualization (in the magician's mind's eye), of the actual object with which the magician wishes these people to become enraptured. This visualization should be exaggerated in the beautiful, enrapturing qualities which the object possesses (but not so much so that it is unacceptable to the minds of the other people). Because their attention has been absorbed by this other object, these people will not notice the magician.

When this form of invisibility can be obtained, one can alter the perceptions which others have of the magician. This is done as follows.

The magician sends out the idea, let us say, that he is handsome. Coupled with this idea, is the slightly exaggerated picture of oneself as handsome (altering whatever physical characteristics are necessary, but not so much so that the picture deviates greatly from reality and is thus not accepted by other people). The people receiving this thought picture will then be hypnotized (or if one is not this successful, their perceptions will be greatly influenced) into viewing the magician as handsome, or anything else he desires.

This same general process can be employed for instilling some deserving person with confidence, or some other quality which he lacks, but desires. The magician sends a thought picture of this person's being confident, etc., into this deserving individual's mind. This person then feels confidence in himself, or any other quality the magician wants him to.

Remember, one must assume the passive state of consciousness before sending any such thought pictures.

Again, it has been slightly difficult to explain this process of influencing other people. However, as one proceeds in his practice, and develops his powers, he will also develop an understanding of how to use this power; for the knowledge of how to apply this power is inherent in the power itself.

## Low Magick and Psychic Attack

In addition to the elaborate operations of Magick, wherein the microcosm joins the marcrocosm, there exist miscellaneous processes of a vulgar nature which also enable the magician to effect change. For example, there is the making of a wax image representative of the person in whom one wishes to effect change and the sticking of pins into this image. Such minor processes are classified as Low Magick because they are based on crude forms of what is called the magical link.

As stated, the microcosm joins the macrocosm during major ceremonies. Under this condition the Mind of the magician becomes the Mind of that Universe and thus directs a force within itself, from a magician within itself, to a target within itself. Thus the direction of the desired force towards the desired target is accomplished easily as a function of Will.[1] In processes of Low Magick the micro-

[1] In a major ceremony the magician disturbs certain conditions in a macrocosm. Certain other conditions must then take place in order to restore the harmony of the cosmos. These changes which in reality the cosmos naturally effects in order to correct its imbalance, are the

cosm does not join the macrocosm, and thus the magician is trying to effect a change in a being which he considers to be something other than himself. Hence there is the need for a link to assure that the magicians force is aimed at, and reaches, the desired target.

In major operations where the microcosm joins the macrocosm, the magician can effect changes of an abstract nature. That is, he can deal with nature as a whole. When he does so, he usually leaves it to the cosmos to effect the change in its own natural way. In processes of Low Magick, however, the magician is dealing with other specific beings and thus he must direct his force towards particular minds. For example, by processes of Low Magick, the magician may be trying to cause pain in another person; or he may be trying to cause some particular person to fall in love with the magician.

In processes of Low Magick, the magician is dealing directly with people's conscious or subconscious minds.[2] The magician deals with people's conscious minds by employing written or spoken language, gestures, etc. Through the use of such communicative links, he may influence people into doing those things which the magician wants done. This is one form of Low Magick.[3]

changes which the magician desired to effect. For example, the magician may create the need in the cosmos for someone to love him. The cosmos will then satisfy this need in order to correct the imbalance created by it.

[2]I here use "subconscious" not only in the psychological sense, but also to mean that part of each person's being which is the sensitive consciousness that accounts for clairvoyance, ESP, etc.

[3]This method should be attempted before one assumes that it is necessary to employ the more complicated processes.

The magician deals with people's sensitive subconscious minds through the process of psychic attack. Psychic attack is of two types. The first type employs a minor physical ceremony in addition to the mental one. The second type employs only the mental ceremony.

In order to illustrate the first type of psychic attack (both physical and mental ceremonies) let us suppose the magician wishes to cause a member of the opposite sex to fall in love with him (or her). In general, the magician must make a wax, or clay, image of the person towards which he wishes to direct his force. The figure should bear as close a likeness to the real person's physical characterisitcs as is within the artistic skill of the magician. Next this image must be consecrated or christened. To do this, the magician takes a purified and consecrated stylus[4] and with it he writes the full name of the desired person on the wax image. As he does this, the magician pronounces the image to be so-and-so (the name of the person). The identification of the image with the actual person is completed by placing the wax image in physical contact with some material object which has been in contact with the desired person. (Thus this object retains forces peculiar to the desired person and allows one to work on the person by working on these forces.) Such objects as could be used are any discarded parts of the desired person's body (locks of hair, nail clippings, etc.) articles of clothing which have been worn by the individual, jewelry which has been

---

[4]The wax, clay, needles, etc., should all be purified and consecrated to their purpose.

worn by the desired person, etc. The image and
the material object which is associated with the
desired individual should be left in contact for the
appropriate number of days.[5] In our present illustration, since this is a process of love, that number of days is seven. After this stage has been completed, the image is, for purposes of Magick, the
actual desired person. The magician now places
(for the same number of days) the wax image in
contact with some material object which has been in
his personal possession and thus contains forces
peculiar to him. The magical link is now complete.
The magician can now direct his love force toward
the desired individual by sticking the wax image
through the heart with a consecrated pin and at the
same time declaring such words as "let so-and-
so's heart develop a great passion for me."

The same general procedure would be followed
to cause misfortune to fall on a person who has in
some way willfully attacked the magician. In this
case, the image and the object associated with the
target person would remain in contact for three
days. There would be no association between the
wax figures and the magician which would correspond to the same act in the previous process.
(This second link is made in operations of love,
friendship, reconciliation, etc. in order to symbolize
the union of the loved ones, or the give and take
between friends. The magician, however, does not
want his force of hatred to attack his enemy and
then be returned; it is to be a one way affair. Therefore, such a second link would not apply to the op-

[5]Based on the nature of the operation as explained in the "System
of Associations."

eration of revenge presently under discussion.)
Lastly, the magician would stick the wax figure
(which is now the actual person) through that part
of the body where he wishes to cause pain in his
enemy. When he does this, the magician states his
purpose aloud in some short declaration. Alternatively, the magician may place the wax figure in a
box which contains evil smelling juices in order to
cause his target person to become ill. Again, a declaration of the purpose is said aloud by the magician. In general, anything which happens to the
consecrated wax figure due to the magician's Will,
will happen to the actual person.

It is essential that the wax or clay figure be
moulded by the magician himself; he cannot purchase a ready-made doll. For it usually takes several
hours to mould such a figure and during all these
hours of work the magician is intently concentrating
his entire force on the image he is constructing.
Also the materials used by the magician in constructing his image must be purified and consecrated
for the same reasons, which were stated in regards
to the construction of the magical instrument.

It must be understood that these physical acts
of moulding an image, creating the physical links,
etc., are only used to aid the magician's concentration. The wax image of the person gives the magician a focal point for his concentration, Imagination and Will. The physical link created in this type
of process is symbolic of the magical link between
the magician's Will and Imagination and the target
person's sensitive subconscious mind.

The actual changes which are effected by such
processes of Low Magick are due to the magician's

influencing the target person's subconscious mind, and then this subconscious mind's influencing the associated conscious mind into feeling love for the magician, fear of a situation, etc. The magician by such minor processes causes illnesses in others much in the same way that psychosomatic illnesses occur naturally in certain individuals. That is, the magician influences the subconscious mind of the target person and this subconscious mind acts through the person's autonomic nervous system to cause bodily conditions such as ulcers, irregularity, aches and pains, etc.

The second type of psychic attack requires greater powers of concentration, Will and Imagination on the part of the magician, for there is here no physical ceremony on which the magician can focus his energies.

The magician attacks deserving individuals in this second manner by first creating out of his Imagination a spirit, a demon, or some kind of monster. Often the magician paces round and round his room, generating more and more energy and continuing to envision the form of his creation. The magician must himself work up all his energies by continuously pacing the floor and filling his creation with the energy he produces by thinking of his hatred for the individual he is about to attack. When the phantasm has absorbed a sufficient amount of energy,[6] it is in control of its further growth. Here the magician completely relaxes and allows his creation to feed on the magician's remaining energies. Finally, the magician loses consciousness. At

---

[6]Fifty-one percent of the magician's total energy.

this same moment the monster gains consciousness and comes into true existence.[7] The Will of the magician (which is the mind of the created demon) then sends the monster to attack the target individual. These creatures which the magician creates are visible to the persons being attacked and to people who are extremely sensitive, but are invisible to all others.

Those people who are attacked in this manner may experience hallucinations (as they term the magician's creations), nightmares, accidents and injuries of all types, sickness, fatigue, etc. This is because the beasts which the magician has created out of his own energies have penetrated these people's subconscious minds and are causing these people to drive themselves insane.

### Metaphysics for the Adeptus Exemptus

### I

When one's consciousness experiences union with God, it is not only the personality which is dissolved, but the entire Creation is annihilated. There are no words involved in this cosmic conscious experience. Only afterwards are words employed in order to try to convey this experience to another. In fact, during the experience there is no such thing as "another," for one is God and thus all and everything. But after the experience, the ego re-emerges and with it re-emerges the Creation and

[7]The demons created by this process are in reality the magician's own entire being of energy which has become polarized towards one objective by the Will and personified by the Imagination.

other egos. Then is the desire to communicate the experience to someone else born. Thus, God says, "The Creation is all an illusion" because from the available words he chooses "illusion" as being the most accurate description.

## II

The God within us is dual. First, He is God. Then, He is God wanting to realize He is God.

In attempting to realize his Godhood, He created the Creation. Now his Creation has asserted itself, in a sense, gotten out of hand. So He tries to organize His Creation once more so that He can realize He is God. But He becomes more and more entangled in His own Creation, until He at last realizes His Creation as His own. Then the Creation is destroyed, leaving only God. Hence, God appears.

> Our world is ours
> Our world is Our God
> Our God is Ours
> We are God.

## III

What does it mean to dream, or to sense reality? Dreams are real. We base our "waking" lives on our dreams; trying to actually attain what in our dreams we already have. Why attain or acquire anything? You can have it all by simply falling asleep.

If, then, a person can satisfy himself through dreaming, why is it that he awakens? The trick is that we never do awaken. When we believe ourselves to be awake we are in fact still dreaming. Truly, we are all the One Consciousness dreaming this dream we call life. We are One Consciousness dreaming the Creation. Thus when we experience ourselves as God, we then call the Creation an illusion. When we awaken we find ourselves as God.

## IV

All contradictions are themselves contradictory (for they make perfect sense). Thus, I throw all of them back upon each other. Black destroys white, and white destroys black, leaving nothingness. Hence time does not exist; space does not exist. Thus God is Omnipresent; God is eternal.

There are many, many words which one has created. Thus there can appear to be many gods, many truths. But in fact, there is One Truth, One God. And He can be experienced when one destroys all the words of the mind.

Now that I have found that we are God, there is no one with whom to share this secret. We all know it.

We cannot even slap our friends on the back, and say, "You and I know it's all a dream." Because our friends are illusions. We are alone.

## V

There is a state wherein the Creation does not exist for God.

There is a state wherein the Creation does exist for God.

When the state of Creation exists, God wishes it did not exist.

When the state of Creation does not exist, God wishes it did exist.

When the state of Creation exists, God is said to by unmanifested, although He still exists as the Creation.

When the state of Creation exists, God wishes it did not exist, so in order to destroy it, He manifests as the Avatar. As the Avatar, he teaches people to realize they are God. He does this because only when all people realize they are Him can He be Whole and One. When God is Whole and One, the Creation no longer exists. Perhaps then another Whim will cause Him to manifest another Creation and begin a new cycle.

## VI

Do not stand below Christ in sorrow and awe. As he was slain so shall you all be slain.

And do not speak of Baba. As he was Silent so shall you all be Silent.

The Avatar is a landmark. He points the way. He indicates which way the Creation has gone, is going, and will go.

Baba was the last Avatar. He was Silent. Again will the universe be Silent when the Creation has ceased.

Baba raises his fingers to his mouth in a sign of Silence, and like one's parents He will blow out the candle of Creation and say "Good night."

## VII

When you die you will realize that you are God, and that everything in your life, including your earthly personality, was your own creation. You will experience yourself as pure consciousness. Thus your earthly death will be the awakening from illusion.

And you will remain the pure consciousness until some gross afterthought of earthly life disturbs your bliss. Then you will once more begin to dream. Thus you will, as we say, live again.

And someday you will die and enter the bliss of pure consciousness. This time there will be no earthly thoughts to act as seeds for dreams, their having been exhausted. Thus you will remain with God eternally.

### Lesser Mysteries

### I

1. Sometimes I kill a cockroach, and sometimes I let it live.

2. A dream is such that as soon as it comes true, it ceases to exist.

3. Gather up the mind, then throw it out!

4. The Tao (Way) is not a road to be traveled; but one who has grasped the eternal Tao leaves the path of Tao behind him no matter which way he moves.

5. Things change, but Change doesn't.

6. The moon appears at the proper time; and the sun descends without argument.

   The sun rises when it is right to do so, and the moon disappears peaceably.

7. There is a man in the desert exclaiming, "I am

terribly hot." Place him on the north pole and he states, "I am terribly cold." He has spoken twice. Is this man a hypocrite and a liar?

8. Being a depository of opposing forces, man is by nature a hypocrite.

9. External conditions influence man's acts and utterances.

10. Man is to develop his consciousness to respond to politics as his skin responds to changes in temperature.

11. That which is soft and yielding may overpower that which is hard and stubborn. Water erodes rock. It is a process involving time.

12. Eternity.
    You can't argue with that.

13. There is no greater truth than that of "everything is."

## II

1. Magick—to effect changes in accordance with Will.

2. Studying Magick, organizes the mind.

3. Further study of Magick, increases one's knowledge.

4. Practice of Magick, one becomes a master of his mind.

5. Master of Magick, one has created a new mind.

6. Place not your faith in the transient and fleeting; but in the eternal.

7. So long as there is the need of faith, you may

supply your own hope. The dead have no need
of prayer.

8. Trust yourself; it is eternal.


### III

1. To become a spiritual man, you must first become a man of the whole world.

2. To become a man of the whole world, you
must first become able to choose the culture in
which you will participate at any one time.

3. When you determine your culture, rather than
your culture determining your view of yourself, you are a man of the whole world.

4. The hands of God do not tremble; but you cannot become God by stopping the twitch in your
hands.

5. First, realize God; thereafter the proper actions
will follow naturally.


### IV

1. Yoga—to unite oneself with the Great Change-
lessness, the One Eternal; so that there united,
one may watch his transient self die, without
fear.

2. All regular intervals are hypnotic. Repetitions
of any kind, such as in meditation, are hypnotic.

3. A thought arises in meditation and is put into

words; afterwards the words are written and spoken out of context. Thus a thought appears totally erroneous (although at the time it may have contained the greatest meaning).

4. The most deeply repressed thought is that of one's death.

5. Realize your death; and your transience and nothingness.

6. And therefrom, act peacefully.

## V

1. Freedom is the right to do what one will provided that in doing so he harms no one other than himself.

2. As the population of a society increases, and each member has to take care not to hurt any other member, freedom decreases.

3. As there are more people in the society, there is a greater likelihood that an act of any one person may hurt another member of society; thus freedom decreases.

4. The psychologist pities the insane with his world of phantoms, demons, vows, and hallucinations. The insane feels for his fellowmen who must cope with traffic lights, police forces, churches and governments.

## VI

1. Write forever—and yet the words would be only repetitions of what has already come from ten thousand other mouths and hands.

*Truths of the Grade of Adeptus Exemptus*

(1)    Many do not believe they are God, because they believe they have problems. They believe that God does not have any problems; so therefore they cannot be God. Yet God does suffer, does love, does feel sorrow, and does know happiness. These are divine emotions which although they exist are overshadowed by eternal divine bliss. But human problems are of impure emotions; it is only necessary for one to see his human problems as illusory, to realize his Godhood.

In the middle of our human personality with its changing situations is the fixed point of God consciousness. We need only sit quietly and witness the fleeting things around us, in order to realize our stability, immortality and Godhood.

(2)    Why must the God-man be celibate, an ascetic and a washer of the poor's feet? When we believe that only such a person is holy, we limit God, who is, in fact, limitless. God exists in everything. He is everything. He dwells in the drunkard and in the lecher. When, in fact, the God-man washes the poor's feet, he is saying to them, "You are God." He is not saying, "I am God."

(3)    If I kill, then I am God sinning; but always I am God.

(4)    Do not doubt what you think you know.

(5)    Things get worse before they get better.

(6)    *We Are Each Ourselves*
The genius awakens;
he takes with him, not one,

not two, but three.
The genius springs to life,
he takes with him, not one million, not two million,
but three million.
The genius shines brightly,
He shines on not one billion, not two billion,
but three billion.
The genius' light grows dim;
dark grow not three billion, not two billion,
but one billion.
The genius plummets to his death,
he takes with him, not three million, not two million,
but one million.
The genius sinks into death,
he takes with him not three, not two, but one.

(7)     *The Magician's Freedom*
Break morals! Destroy tradition!
havock, chaos, rampant sedition!
Away with customs! Defy ethics!
Dry sands, wet floods, spreading confusion.
Quickly act; or leave it to fate.
Get drunk, make love, or else meditate
No right, no wrong, so do what you will!
Build up, destroy, but don't imitate.

Always good, then spread corruption!
Sinning, grinning, exquisite seduction.
Leap Imagination, and expose the fools
No proofs, no truths, for sure nothing's known.

(8)     We are immortal! What foolishness for anyone
to think we are not. Where does one intend to go
when he dies?

(9)     Don't wish for anything. You already have
what you truly want, and you know it!

(10)   Everyday the hermit mystic proves to us that life is meaningless. He does this by sitting on the side and wasting his life.

(11)   He had suffered much, this sorrowful, sorrowful man. Now in the hopes of receiving some spiritual comfort, he made pilgrimage to the great mystic. Sitting at the wise one's feet, he recounted, with tears in his eyes and amidst much sobbing, his tales of hardship and suffering. Then the great mystic turned to this sad and pitiable creature and shouted, "If you don't like living, kill yourself!"

(12)   And it will appear that I have become crazy, though, in fact, I will have only begun to realize the Truth.

(13)   Everyone gets what they deserve. Social problems are due to the people's apathy and laziness. There is no reason for anyone to accept things as they are, except that they value security more than anything else. There is no reason for anyone to remain poor—if I were poor I would take a chance at becoming a master thief; not a common, petty thief, but a master thief. But most would rather remain poor and curse it.

(14)   The man who has nothing to lose is the most dangerous man alive.

(15)   Do not listen to oratorial revolutionaries, those who only talk, but are termed revolutionaries by the mass media. A real revolutionary must carry a gun. He knows that the ultimate, real power is actual destructive power. Only threats to a rigid person's well-being can cause him to change. But most would rather hope for change than fight for it.

(16)    Everyone wants peace, but few are willing to make the sacrifices. Yet as long as there are millionaires living alongside people who are starving, there will be no peace.

(17)    Entering the Abyss.

## XI

## THE ABYSS

### *You Are Doomed*

What is it like to be doomed? It is knowing that no matter what you do, you are trapped. It is knowing that there are things you want which you can never have. These are not material things which exist out there; these are not external objects which you can scheme or go after, and one day touch and hold. I will not tell you what it is you truly want; I can say only that you are doomed to never have it. You can run into the world and try to drown yourself in its amusements; you can retreat to a mountain and meditate; you can drink and take drugs; you can plead with others to tell you, to aid you, to help you; or you can kill yourself—but none of these will bring release, liberation, or enlightenement. You are doomed.

Now certain philosophers will tell you that the only answer to this dilemma is to compromise, to make the best you can of this predicament called life. But at best, this is temporary appeasement; it is not freedom. You are doomed.

And there are other philosophers, old and wise, who have spent their lives trying to divine the answer to this problem. Some believe they have succeeded, but believe me, they have only examined the situation, discussed the problem, and enumerated the issues; theirs is no answer—it is only a description of the dilemma. You are doomed.

# XII

## THE GRADE OF MAGISTER TEMPLI

### Truth Absolute

#### I

Without the mystical experience, Truth Absolute cannot be understood.

He who knows the Absolute Truth cannot communicate it to another, but may give advice as an aid to another so that he may experience the Truth for himself.

Truth Absolute is One and eternal, but the advice which will aid an individual may be different and numerous. Therefore, a searcher for Truth, when he confronts He who knows the Truth, may receive a certain advice, but everyone else must realize that this advice was given solely to that other individual, and under special conditions.

Another individual may ask He who knows the Truth the same question, but receive a different answer. Two or more different answers may come from the One Eternal Truth, because He who knows the Truth knows that the different searchers have different needs; the different searchers are at different stages of consciousness evolution and thus require answers appropriate to their individual advancement.

Therefore, when he who knows the Truth advises a searcher after Truth, mankind must not assume that this answer applies to them as a whole. There can be no sects based on inflexible rules. A searcher after Truth may be told by He who knows the Truth to refrain from eating. The teacher may do this in order that the aspirant experience fasting, for he knows that it is necessary for this aspirant to experience fasting at this time. This advice should not become the basis for a rule requiring fasting by all other aspirants.

Thus in the world, there are only truths, that is, individual advices which are correct for certain individuals. Truth Absolute transcends the world.


## II

Truth is unlimited and absolute.

Words are finite and subject to interpretation. Therefore, Truth cannot be expressed in words. But words can help lead one towards experiencing the Truth.


## II

Truth is eternal and absolute.

The world is transient and finite.

Thus, Truth cannot be applied to the world. But when circumstances are specifically stated, the Absolute Truth can state what is correct in that particular case by applying one aspect of itself.

### The Life of Magick

I. To All Who Are Capable of Understanding

1. As Man you are born into Society.

2. As it is your Duty to preserve your Life; and as Society will destroy you if you do not comply with its Demands; you must act as Society demands—this regardless of your Inclinations.

3. You are free to pursue your Pleasures, but if discovered must suffer the Consequences. The way to avoid Discovery is to moderate your Desires.

4. Always Man must obey Society; but if that Society becomes corrupt, or asks of Man that he do that which is prohibited by the Divine, then all Notions of Right and Wrong are suspended; and if Man then angers and fights to alter or destroy Society, so be it.

II. To the Insane, Incapable of Understanding

1. Though his Body might be in Chains, Man's Mind is always free.

2. But let not this Thought appease One, for it is Action which affirms Life.

3. And again, if his actions be restricted, let him not fear the overwhelming Expansion of his Imagination. For then though he be subjected to Many Trials, he shall not care. Yes, though he be recalled by all the world, he shall not return.

4. Then shall it become Society's Duty to care for he whom it has chased away.

5. And if this Society fails to do; then this too shall be counted among Society's Sins.

III. To the Few Capable of Realization

1. To fulfill Society's Demands and yet to realize the Freedom of the Mind; this is the Life of Reason and also Mysticism.

2. To succeed in both Reason and Mysticism; this is Magick.

### The Material World and the Magical World

I

Through Magick, one becomes his Ideal Being, his God, God. In this, his own newly created position, he may re-order the world from which he originally took his images and thoughts of ideals. Thus through Magick one uses the present existing world to alter himself and become God, so that after having attained this, he may create a new world. Into this new world he places (and omits) what he wishes. However we must in Magick distinguish most carefully from what is true and what is false.

When beginning the practice of Magick, the materialist world is referred to as the True World and the magic world is referred to as the False World. However, when due to a magical operation we are situated in our "False World" we then refer to the world of magic as True and the materialist world as False. In other words, the world which one inhabits at the time of reference is the True World.

After having traveled to and from one's two worlds a number of times, one realizes the above mentioned relativism. It is this knowledge of relativism which has caused a "k" to be placed at the end of the standard word "magic." The "k" is an afterthought that points to the fact that one realizes that the preceding magic is not the whole Truth.

As analogy, one lives with no thought of dying, although reason tells one he will die. From the moment of truly realizing one's inevitable death, one's actions are restrained by this knowledge. The thought is then repressed so that one may again live as if he would never die. This process continues ad infinitum. It is similar to dreaming the impossible dream, although one knows it is impossible. It also is similar to acting, although one knows all actions are fruitless. Just so in Magick the thought of magick's "falseness"[1] must be kept in mind by the Master even whilst he employs it. This process has been called "controlled folly."

The True and False are two worlds; and one, when cultivating his False World through magic, must always be careful not to allow the two worlds to merge. No one factor must leave the False World of magic and enter the True World of materialism.

In Magick, the god one becomes and the world one creates is the True World, but only for oneself. If it should find its way into the False World of Materialism and be accepted there, then it is possible to truly create a new world (on earth).

Thus Magick, is a technique which can be explained by such means as this writing, and which is

[1]Magick does work, but not due to the publicly stated reasons.

a common tool for all to use, but the magician may employ this one method to create an infinite number of Worlds.

The Master is one who has constructed his own True World, but realizes that others may view it as false. The Master must further realize the separation of magic from that which magic creates. The symbols of Magick are vehicles to reach a certain state of consciousness wherein he creates his True World; but these symbols must not then, in any way, be thought of as being that universe.

Situated in one's True World (the world which is false to all others) one may come to possess certain knowledge. This knowledge can be useful to one in his actions in his False World (to the magician, the materialist world). But this can only be so if the Master realizes the barrier between the two worlds and generalizes the knowledge so that it fits and may be transported via the symbols common to both worlds. Understand too, that generalizing the transcendental knowledge results in distortion; so that when anyone speaks of the world of magic via language little is really expressed.

Magick is the leaving point of one's False World and the beinning of one's True World. Thus Magick is a part of both worlds. It not only is a bridge between two worlds, but extends slightly into each.

The Void traversed by the bridge is called the Abyss. Notice that the aspirant views the bridge as a path leading up to another world and calls that bridge "magic"; whereas the Master looks back on that bridge as the vehicle by which he came and calls that bridge "Magick."

As his journey depends on faith, the aspirant

may be thought of as walking up the bridge backwards. The half-way point on the bridge where the
aspirant must do an about-face is the Abyss of
Abysses. Here he may walk back down the bridge,
taking a portion of the magical knowledge available to him; or he may continue walking up the
bridge backwards (that is, still facing the False
World of materialism). In this case, the aspirant is
leaving his False World behind for he knows not
what—because he has not as yet viewed his True
World. If the aspirant does walk down the bridge
from the Abyss of Abysses, he is hereafter referred
to as a Brother of the Left-hand Path. If he continues across the remainder of the Abyss, the aspirant
is referred to as a Brother of the Right-hand Path.

The Brother of the Left-hand Path is not truly
evil as he is habitually represented. His troubles,
and those of the world, are due to that he only
possesses a portion of Truth. This portion of Truth
when brought down the bridge and applied to the
aspirant's False World (the common material world)
causes the aspirant to think and behave in ways
that are not understood by others and are termed
evil.

The Brother of the Right-hand Path is generally thought of as possessing the opposite qualities
—goodness, kindness, charitableness. He must create
and master his True World and start to acquire the
knowledge necessary for transporting his noble
ideas to his False World. This is the work for the
Master-of-the-Temple.

The Magus is one who has acquired all magical
(transcendental) knowledge and has succeeded in

conveying a worthy percentage of it to his False World (the common materialist world).

## II

The physically true and the physically possible.

That which is always physically possible may at any time become physically true. When such a physically possible phenomenon enters the world of the physically true a number of times, we cease referring to it as physically possible, and realize it as being physically probable.

a) The Will is to the physically true as the Imagination is to the physically possible.

The world of magic is one of the Imagination. However, through Will one may physically create that which once existed only in one's Imagination. Thus the Will is the vehicle and energy which enables one to bring the real physical world into accordance with one's Imagination. The method by which the Will alters reality so that it conforms with Imagination is Magick.

One practice of Magick will serve as an example. The aspirant studies all that he may concerning a god who exhibits qualities which the aspirant wishes to attain. That is, he saturates his Imagination with thoughts and images of this god. Next, the aspirant through Will brings his life into accordance with that of the divine being. In this practice, he acts as would the god he is trying to become. So that the aspirant may succeed in this practice, the Will is further strengthened by a technique named "the assumption of the god-form." The assumption of the god-form is performed by the aspirant's assuming a posture and guise which has come to be identified with the god in question. Concentrating severely, he then visualizes himself living as though he were the god under study.

b) All things which can be thought of are possible. Those things which cannot be thought of are impossible.

It has been said that it is possible to dream the impossible dream. This immediately points to a contradiction—for if it can be thought of, it is not truly impossible. Such improbable dreams are termed impossible due to an underestimation of the power of the Will and/or the Imagination. It is the purpose of Magick to strengthen the Will, and to develop and free the Imagination. With a freer Imagination, one may create solutions to problems and begin to understand ideas which were puzzling.

But there is a limit to the Imagination, for the Imagination creates new concepts by selecting and re-combining already known ideas. Thus, for instance, it is truly impossible to imagine a new color. One may close his eyes, but try as he might, he cannot visualize a new color—for he will try to create this new color by combining known colors and will thereby arrive only at known hues.

c) Many stagger at the impossibility of thinking in terms of an infinite universe. In fact, it is impossible to close one's eyes and visualize an infinite universe, and therefore such a universe does not exist. But let me now illustrate how the Imagination can allow one to understand concepts which were previously confounded by formulating a story based on the problem.

It is said that the universe is boundless, it can come to no end because always on the other side of the border is space, and thus the universe continues endlessly. But matter and space are but energy. The various forms of matter and space are due to energies vibrating at different rates. Because energies are vibrating at different rhythms, we (because we too are composed of vibrating energies) perceive differentiations and thus the world of different objects and space. In truth, there is no matter and space, but only Energy. The universe is an ocean of Energy. You do not think of this ocean as infinite, because when all there is, is Energy, there is no space and matter; and thus no thought of the Infinite.

Time is a relation between the movement of matter in space. When all is realized as Energy and there is therefore no matter and space, it follows that there can be no time.

It is to the mind that time, space, and matter do not exist.

d) Many stagger at the impossibility of discovering how and why the universe was created. Religions are stories formulated by Imaginations in order to appease human curiosity. In fact, what happens when we die, is that we die. *But this too is a story!*

### Meditations for the Magister Templi

### I

Assume a relaxed lying position. Next, purposefully recount in one's mind's eye, various scenes from one's past. Do not stop to consider the meaning of any of these past experiences. Instead, push the mind quickly from one scene to another. Do not stop to consider chronological order. Instead, visualize in the mind's eye one incident after another in rapid succession. As one becomes exhausted in this exercise, one becomes detached from these past experiences. Feel the unreality of these past incidents. Realize the dream-like nature of these images of the past. Will tomorrow's events be just such dreams?

## II

Having successfully traversed the Abyss, the Magister Templi must now renounce all that he ever was. He must break with the past while he is stripped of his attainments. Accordingly, the Magister Templi must destroy old mementos and other reminders of the past, such as photographs, letters, etc. If it is practical and safe to do so, he should burn these items in an open fire so that he may observe their destruction.

If the Magister Templi should fail in this final task, he will be returned to the sufferings of the Abyss. He will become a Brother-of-the-Left-hand Path, and will in time be consumed by insanity or worse.

### The Truths of the Grade of Magister Templi

(1) The Magister Templi is the expression of his True Will. All his actions and thoughts reflect his True Will.

(2) The Magister Templi must teach the way to enlightenment.

(3) The student must be made to do extensive read-

ing of the theories in the systems of attainment, in order that he discover that his salvation resides in none of the sacred writings.

(4) The Magister Templi must guide the aspirant in his practices.

(5) Forget yourself.

(6) He who desires anything cannot be free. He who desires freedom cannot be free.

(7) There are no secrets in the East. There are no secrets in the West. The Truth is within.

(8) There is no future, until it comes; then it is the present.

There is no past, only present memories.

(9) He who doesn't know, doesn't speak.

He who doesn't know, but believes otherwise— he speaks much and finds it easy.

He who truly knows finds it difficult to speak, and does so sparingly.

(10) Everyone wants to believe in something. But I believe in nothing, and yet go on living.

(11) Each mind is itself and as such cannot be known to any other mind. Therefore, you know of no mind other than your own. However, you may infer from the physical actions of other human bodies that they have a mind similar to your own. But what you know of another's mind is subjective; this knoweldge is always distorted by one's own mind. Knowledge of another's mind is nothing more than knowledge of one's own mind projected into another's body.

Truly, the world exists only in one's own mind. Therefore, to change one's world, it is only necessary to alter one's own mind. For if one suspects another of doing evil although the overt act indicates othewise, one is attributing his own selfish motives to another. Likewise, another may appear to be acting wickedly when in fact his act is merciful and stems from compassion.

When through Magick we annihilate personal desires, we no longer suspect others of harboring evil motives. Then, one can attune oneself with the Universal Mind, and know intuitively the minds of others.

(12) A berry which thinks itself sweet, will taste so to others.

(13) Having comprehended the Absolute Truth, there are but two things one might say. Firstly, one may not speak at all, silence being the expression of the Truth. Secondly, one may speak whenever one wants and whatever one wishes. This will involve stating contradictions, which neutralizing each other will result in saying nothing. In the second case one never considers justifying his actions, although his words may indicate differently. For at different times and under different conditions, one may differently justify one's actions. Thus, these contradictions or evidences of illogical thinking, result in stating nothing—which is what is done in the first case. However, of these two expressions of Truth, the first one, that of literally not speaking, is the best, for there is less chance of one's being misunderstood. In the case of saying everything regardless of contradictions, one is still supplying material which others may meditate upon, analyze, and so

confuse themselves into believing they have found the Truth.

(14) He turned to the great mystic and said, "What you don't say is absolutely correct."

(15) Eternity.
  You can't argue with that!

(16) Truly imagine what it would be like to have one's every wish come true as soon as it is wished, almost before one wishes it. What a bore! There would be very little satisfaction. To struggle is man's fate.

(17) Truly imagine what it would be like to live forever, and do not wish for immortality. Without death, life would be meaningless.

(18) My life is a joke. But when I die, I won't be around to laugh.

(19) When you catch up to yourself, the mind stops. That's it—enlightenment!

# XIII

## THE GRADE OF MAGUS

### *The Book of Life and Death*

I      I am God.

II      Regard me as the Two-fold God; the God of Life and the Living; the God of Death and the Dead.

III      First; the God of Life and the Living.

IV      Know you that you are alive.

V      You shall not kill.

VI      You shall not steal.

VII      With understanding and observance of these two commandments, do whatever you will.

VIII      In Life, you are each different.

IX      Each man is destined to find pleasure and happiness in a different way.

X      Save that he violates either of the two commandments, judge not the thoughts or actions of another man; for this I shall do for him.

| XI | Act intelligently and compassionately towards all beings. |
|---|---|
| XII | Or assume responsibility for doing harm. |
| XIII | I shall manifest unto you when it pleases me; nay, when it pleases you. |
| XIV | I shall deliver my power unto you as I divine your need; nay, as you divine your need. |
| XV | There is nothing which is not me. |
| XVI | All thoughts shall be created unto me; and all actions shall be done with reverence unto me. |
| XVII | In all you do, you shall do for me. |
| XVIII | And I shall be forever with you. |
| XIX | Think only of the happiness and of the pleasures of the life which I have given you. |
| XX | All sorrows will pass and be reconciled. |
| XXI | The unbeliever's life will be his Hell. |

| I | Second; the God of Death and the Dead. |
|---|---|
| II | Know you that you will die. |
| III | Consider this once, and not again. |
| IV | Let not the thought of death enter life. |
| V | Know you that in death you are each the same. |
| VI | If you have lived as I have asked, you will then find eternal bliss. |

VII        Life is to be lived. Do not hasten with your
           own hand that which I shall have power
           over.

VIII       I cause you to seek me; yet refrain from em-
           bracing you; this so that our reunion at
           last shall be of complete bliss. Await me with
           your death!

IX         Search; and you shall find the eternal, though
           you are alive. But never until death will you
           remain long to rest with me. Bless me, that
           this I refuse you.

X          Yearn to know me; but not to become me.

XI         To know the eternal whilst still alive is a
           happiness of life. But to become the eternal
           to escape life, is death; though the body
           may live on.

XII        Tell no one of your stumbles and hard-
           ships to reach me. These shall remain un-
           known and hidden to aid those I love, and
           hinder those I despise.

XIII       Through thoughts and actions you seek me
           out so that you may catch me before I may
           catch you; you cannot win; nor can you
           lose. Await me with your death!

XIV        Know you that you are eternal, and shall
           have life ten thousand times until you are
           able to live the life of truth and happiness.

*The Truths of the Grade of Magus*

(1)  Absolute True Knowledge is knowledge which
is not based on sensory experience; but on the direct
experience of consciousness.

(2) God in the highest, most original condition is a state of non-existence in which the potential for existence is latent. With the manifestation of this urge to exist, the Creation was born. Do not ask why this act occurred; it is the whim of God. A whim cannot be explained; if this were the case it would be a reason, and not a whim.

(3) Being and Non-being (and other such so-called dualities) may exist at the same time. This cannot be understood logically, but it is true. Such "dualities" do exist at the same time, because there is neither existence nor non-existence.

(4) In the beginning—ONE. There was neither Being nor Non-being. It is only now that one can say "In the beginning, *there was* ONE." There was neither Being nor Non-being, for neither can exist without the other. Therefore, neither Being nor Non-being was born out of the other. As soon as there is either Being or Non-being the other instantly appears.

Thought gives rise to Being. It is, therefore, impossible to think of Non-being. In order to know Non-being, the cessation of thought is necessary. This is accomplished by a system of attainment.

(5) Some of the Enlightened, say "Do this, and become Enlightened." Other Enlightened say, "Do that, and become Enlightened." Still other Enlightened say, "Do neither this nor that, but instead do this and become Enlightened." By whose right do these various systems come into being? Is there anyone who is truly Enlightened? Yes, there are those who are Enlightened, but their Enlightenment was not the conscious result of any practice of any

discipline. All Enlightenment stems from some un-known cause. Perhaps this unknon factor is some-thing common to all systems of attainment? No, All Enlightenement is a miracle, just as all the Cre-ation is a miracle.

(6) Everyone must desire Enlightenment. But any-one who thinks they can attain Enleightenment, cannot attain Enlightenment. Enlightenment comes.

(7) When one seeks after something, one seeks his identity. In seeking something, one defines himself in terms of the other thing. In defining oneself, one limits oneself. The Enlightened one is not limited. Therefore do not seek, but know.

(8) Does Absolute Truth contain mistakes?

(9) Pain is pain, but it is not Evil.

(10) One who knows the Truth, lives neither in the world nor the monastery, but in the Truth.

(11) He who is last will be first. But he who knows this, and so purposely places himself last in order to be first, will remain last.

(12) Knowledge is power. Ignorance is bliss. En-lightment is where both of these meet.

(13) When the mind catches up to itself—that's en-lightenment.

(14) Truth is the silent and invisible basis from which springs all falsehoods.

# XIV

## THE GRADE OF IPSSISSIMUS

### *The Magic Maze*

The maze of magic is a magic maze,
With all its secrets obscured by an haze,
So thick and cloudy, that only the most discerning
    eye,
Can pierce it, with the point of a triangular lie.
To try, try, and to try again,
And learn that it's pointless to ever try again;
This is the end to thought that brings release,
The end to pursuit, with one's mind at ease.
Never there was a demon, an angel, or thought,
It was only within one's own self were we caught;
The world was a maze run by human mice,
And the realm of magic, a fool's paradise.

### *Truths of the Grade of Ipssissimus*

(1)  For the Grade of Ipssissimus, only a few clues
     are given.

(2)  Although there is no I, I am Absolute Truth.

(3)  Although there is no I, I am Being.

(4)  How does it feel to be an echo?
     I am only an echo.

(5)  I have stood in front of people without their hav-
     ing seen me.

(6)   All texts are only so much words.

(7)   All words are out of context. They are out of context of the Truth.

(8)   All hypothetical probelms are false, for they are limiting. It is a waste to consider them.

(9)   All beliefs are true to the believer; therefore let each man say "I know."

(10) Life is but a dream.
Death does not exist.
Reality is awakening.

(11) Reality and fantasy—I see the difference, and there is none.

(12) All matter is unreal. There is no duality.

(13) The Mind and Body are One.

(14) Everything is not caused.

(15) There is no free will; nor is there determinism. There is no time.

(16) Everything is One, yet each thing is different. There is only One, yet each thing is itself.

(17) Everything is exactly as it should be; and everyone is doing exactly what he should be doing. It cannot be otherwise.

(18) The moon is not silver.
The sun's rays are reflected from its surface.

(19) I neither believe nor disbelieve anything.

(20) When someone dies, someone is being born.

(21) The world doesn't care about me, And I don't care about the world.

I say to it, "Don't mind me. I'm just passing through."

And the world is also just passing through.

In fact, the process of passing through is just passing through itself.

(22) All actions are fruitless.

(23) It is impossible for anyone to prove anything to anyone else.

(25) In the end, this creation will not exist. There is, therefore, no great purpose or goal for anyone to pursue. Even the names of famous people will be nothing, for all recorded history will not exist. There will be no people to read of any past.

To realize the above fully, and not only intellectually, releases one from any anxiety regarding his frantic pursuits. There is no need to fear not completeing some important task. Do not be nervous or apprehensive as regards dying before having made any great discovery. But understand that this realization does not result in inactivity; rather, it results in tranquillity regardless of activity. This realization is known as the elimination of the martyr complex.

Thus is one allowed to die peacefully and without regret.

In the end, all the actions of everyone will amount to nothing.

(25) The Ipssissimus must keep silent as regards his initiation into this Grade. He must draw himself behind a veil, and live as an ordinary man.